A SHARP CRIME MYSTERY

A MATTER OF TIME

Diane M. McPhee

BLUE FORGE PRESS

Port Orchard ✱ Washington

A Matter of Time
Copyright 2025
by Diane M. McPhee

First eBook Edition November 2025
First Print Edition November 2025

ISBN 979-8-89439-063-5

For information about film, reprint or other subsidiary rights, contact: blueforgegroup@gmail.com

Blue Forge Press is the print division of the volunteer-run, federal 501(c)3 nonprofit, Blue Legacy (EIN 83-4307421), founded in 1989 and dedicated to supporting artisans marginalized due to race, age, disability, economics or other factors. We strive to empower storytellers from all walks of life with our four divisions: Blue Forge Press, Blue Forge Films, Blue Forge Gaming, and Blue Forge Sound. Find out more at www.BlueForgeGroup.org

Blue Forge Press
7419 Ebbert Drive Southeast
Port Orchard, Washington 98367
blueforgepress@gmail.com
360-550-2071 ph.txt

ACKNOWLEDGMENTS

Researching gangs, housing projects, and drugs in a big city was complex and disturbing. I read about gangs using children as lookouts while engaging in brazen criminal activity, along with the poverty and fragile structure of the housing projects and the people who live there. Learning about the complicated circumstances of disadvantaged groups also led me to acknowledge the significant efforts law enforcement plays each day when handling the ongoing calls and trying to improve community relations. I hope I put policework in a positive light.

Thank you to my readers who have followed Detective Alan Sharp along his investigations. I wanted to portray a man who followed old school rules and who appreciated his colleagues and friends who were trying to make a difference and keep citizens safe. I also enjoyed writing about his struggles with technology because I have had to call my children to learn how to set reminders or to explain the way to navigate the apps I seldom use. Like Alan, I still use paper and pen to make lists and notes to myself.

My thanks also go to Blue Forge Press who always remain supportive and encouraging.

A Matter of Time

Diane M. McPhee

MONDAY, OCTOBER 2nd

Detective Alan Sharp walked carefully along the leaf strewn path of the Boston Common and reminded himself that nothing stays the same... everything changes. The colorful New England fall had been gorgeous this year, but the leaves had started to fall, and the grounds and walkways were often left a slimy mess. The city of Boston faithfully sent their troops out to clear the paths and streets, but it was a thankless task until all the leaves cleared the trees. *That would be another week or two,* Alan thought. He was careful to watch his step.

It was nothing new for Alan to dislike change because he hated to shift out of the known and into the unknown. He chided himself because change wasn't going away just because he was resistant to it. What was that old saying about the only constant in life is change? Alan had to smile to himself thinking about that. He knew he didn't have to love change or embrace it, just modify his feelings and behaviors in the face of uncertainty. After all, people change, develop habits and move on to better or different environments. And the universal truth was that every challenge makes life a little more interesting. Another old adage he suspected.

Alan was not looking forward to what was on his schedule today. His partner, Detective Enrique Mendez, was leaving the department, and this was his last day. They had been partners for over seven years and relied on each other's skills and, most importantly, friendship and trust. What would Alan do without him? How were they going to wrap things up after all this time? Enrique was due to meet with him first thing this morning.

Alan approached the station and slowly climbed the several steps, holding on to the handrail for support. He had developed some arthritis in his right knee and tried to ignore the weakness in his thigh muscle. This was a change he didn't want to accept. His doctor told him that for a man of his age, he should be pacing his activities throughout the day. He even suggested that a walking stick may be beneficial. This made Alan even more determined to park his car away from the precinct and walk through the Commons before work. After all, he was only sixty-eight years old, which people now considered to be middle aged.

Because Alan's office was located at the back of the unit, most of the detectives on duty looked up and nodded as he passed through. Alan overheard a couple of his officers leaning back in their chairs arguing about a witness they wanted to shake up or was a waste of time and he noticed several guys with the phone pressed to one ear. They all appeared to avoid Alan's presence because they knew this was the day Detective Mendez would be signing off. Most of them were aware of the friendship the two men had for each other and knew it was going to be a tough day.

At exactly 9:00, Detective Enrique Mendez walked through the station and entered Alan's office. He was dressed in his regular attire for work, a dark navy suit, a light blue button-down shirt and a funny tie. His three girls loved giving him unusual ties and this one had sailboats drifting through. It was one of his favorites.

Alan noticed how tired his friend locked and imagined it was because of the upheaval his family was experiencing. Making any transition from familiar safety to something new and uncertain, was a challenge. Enrique sat quietly on the chair beside Alan's desk and brought out his notebook. "I guess I don't know how we're going to do this. I've spoken to the captain, and everything's in order for me to sign off. What can I do for you?"

Alan smiled and looked fondly at his partner. "Tell me again where you're going."

Enrique shook his head and laughed. "That seems to be the question of the hour. Marie all the sudden bought a plane ticket to visit her family in New Mexico for a week. I'll stay here to take the girls to school and events." At this point Enrique shook his head and smiled slightly. "I think they're already worried about my being in charge because I've seen them roll their eyes when they talk with their mother." The Mendez girls were devoted to their parents and were probably trying to understand the transition they were witnessing.

"So, then what…?" Alan wanted to hear his friend's entire plan.

Enrique continued while rubbing his right shoulder. "You know I haven't been a hundred percent since I got shot in my shoulder. The pain has reached my arm and affected my hand so now I need to rely on my left hand for most things. So, I've been taking some sophisticated computer classes and found out I'm good at coding and research. I've been hired for a job in Seattle with Google. You're the first to know." Enrique smiled, hoping this would please Alan.

"Seattle! I can visit you when I go to see my daughter! This is better news than I thought!" Alan's daughter, Lindsay, lived in a suburb of Seattle along with her husband and twin boys. "When do you leave?"

"When Marie gets back, we'll pack up. Google moves us and even offers a bonus. We've rented a house near the city, and the girls are already enrolled in a private school. It all seems to be moving fast."

Alan looked at his watch. "Let's have lunch in a couple hours and you can tell me more. I have the final interview for a recruit, a detective in fact, coming in shortly. Do you want to stick around?"

"No... you can tell me all about it over lunch." Enrique stood and offered a hand to his partner. Alan came around the desk and held out his arms to hug the man who stood with him for more dangerous cases than they would care to remember.

Vivian Collins had passed the detective exam over a year ago from the Connecticut Public Safety Training Academy. She had served for several years on patrol in the city of Hartford and had been encouraged to move forward in her field. It had been an arduous journey since she was raising a teenage daughter who seemed to need her constant attention while questioning her mother's every move and decision. To get regular hours and keep an eye on her daughter, Vivian had requested to be assigned to cold cases when she became a detective. Although the cold cases kept her busy, she realized how much she missed working with the public. When she saw the opportunity to apply for the detective position in Boston, she jumped on it.

Vivian was now waiting for a formal interview with Detective Alan Sharp. His reputation was widely known and respected. He didn't just mouth platitudes of hard work like attention to detail, loyalty and drive, he lived them. Vivian had heard that officers were inspired by Detective Sharp and considered him a role model. She also heard that he toed the line. He was traditional and expected his officers to follow the main Constitutional Amendments that applied to the duties of a law enforcement officer. These laws safeguarded citizen's rights while providing clear guidelines regarding the proper use of power. It was Detective Sharp's golden rule that an officer cannot use any evidence in an individual criminal case if they violate one or more of these constitutional rights. Vivian faithfully adhered to these rules and policies and hoped to include this when speaking to the detective. She would do anything to secure a position on the Boston force.

Alan had interviewed several candidates for the detective position and was still uncertain. He knew he was feeling the loss of Enrique and compared each interviewee with Enrique's years of service. Detective Vivian Collins was his last prospect, and he was uncertain about her. Her references were outstanding, but her experience was limited to mainly cold cases. Alan was aware that references were mainly positive endorsements, vouching for the candidate's personality, character and attributes. Sometimes he wondered if the person themselves had written these letters. He usually made his best decisions when he could meet the candidate eye to eye, ask some open-ended candid questions, and see if he could gauge how they might fit into the busy precinct. He rang the officer in charge to have Detective

A MATTER OF TIME

Collins escorted into his office.

When Vivian walked in, Alan stood to shake her hand. He first noticed how short her hair was, cut close to her well-shaped head, accentuating her dark eyes and cinnamon brown complexion. She was slim and shorter than Alan's 5'11"... but not by much.

Vivian nodded and in a low, raspy voice said, "Thank you for the opportunity to apply to the position. Shall we begin?"

Alan liked this directness and pointed to the chair in front of his desk. He decided to begin with a new approach. "What have you learned recently?"

Vivian was surprised by such a candid question. She had expected the regular queries about job, motivation and future. She sat back further into her chair and thought for a minute. "Last year, my precinct went fully remote. It was a big change for some of us, especially the older officers." She looked up, hoping she hadn't offended her superior. She then continued, "After a few days of trials and errors, I emailed those who I knew were struggling like I was and asked them to meet for a video call. We invited our computer tech to join us, and we all spent valuable time learning ways to come up with a daily system and to navigate our intel. While working with others who kept asking important questions, I believe I learned more in those hours than I had in years."

Alan smiled and asked another unusual question. "What is your work style?"

Again, Vivian was surprised by the question. She glanced to the right of Alan and thought for more than a minute. She then set a determined look on her face and said, "I believe that open debate and discussion are vital to progress and innovation when working with a team, sir, and I always allow room for constructive criticism and new ideas." Vivian shifted in her chair. "I suppose this tendency can sometimes make me appear confrontational at times, and sometimes I might be perceived as being too opinionated... but I think we need strong voices to move forward to create positive change." Vivian offered a flash of a smile. She continued, "I have respect for the officers I have worked with and supported their insights and will always advocate for them when I believe they're right."

Alan nodded. He liked her. She was outspoken and expressed strong opinions very directly. He wondered if it would be difficult to change her mind even in the face of evidence that contradicts her beliefs. It would be a challenge.

"What motivates you, Detective Collins?"

Vivian nodded slowly. "I have a teenage daughter who motivates and challenges me every day. I keep reminding her that we're in this life together and to try our best to work as a team. As for my job, making a difference in the lives of families motivates me to strive for excellence in everything I do. I always work towards getting a positive outcome that might change lives and increase public trust in our uniform."

Alan glanced at Vivian's profile on his desk. She was thirty-six and single. "You're living in Hartford and, I assume, you would have to move if you got this job. Is that a problem?"

Vivian felt encouraged. "No... not at all. I have a sister who lives in Brighton and has offered us her basement until we can find a place to move. My daughter's enrolled in online classes now and can sign up with a neighboring school for ongoing lessons."

A MATTER OF TIME

Alan asked Vivian some more typical questions about her last job. He was interested in the cold cases she had worked on but didn't want to go into much detail until he made the decision to hire her. When the hour was up, he walked her to the door and shook her hand. "It was very nice speaking with you. I'll be deciding soon and will get back to all the candidates."

Vivian smiled and said, "I would like the opportunity to work with you, Detective Sharp. I'm sorry to hear you are losing your partner after all the years working together. Sometimes change is a good thing... for all of us."

As she walked away, Alan appreciated the advice. He was going to remember this when he met with Enrique for lunch.

Enrique was waiting at the Pub around the corner from the station. He and Alan liked the atmosphere in that restaurant along with the meals offered. When Alan came rushing in the door, Enrique had to laugh. His friend was always late.

"Sorry," Alan began, "I just had to jot down some notes before I met you." He noticed the smile on Enrique's face. "I know what you're thinking... late as usual."

The waiter approached them, and they both ordered cokes and burgers. They didn't need to look at a menu to know what was good.

"How did the last interview go?" Enrique was curious.

"I liked her. She seemed confident and a bit outspoken, but maybe that might shake things up a bit. I've interviewed six other candidates, and I think she's the best."

"You know," Enrique grinned, "it's always an advantage to be the last one interviewed. Especially if you're just as qualified as the other candidates. It's some psychological truth. So, tell me what else you like about her."

"She's a single mom and has a teenage daughter. I'd like to think she understands the younger generation and could be a valuable source of support, insight and inspiration dealing with that age group. That would be a bonus for our aging department. She also appears energetic and best of all, curious."

"And the cons…" Enrique knew Alan well. He never decided without looking at both sides of a coin.

Alan smiled. "I think she needs to allow room for constructive criticism and tried and true ways of handling cases. That's just my opinion. Now tell me more about your move."

The men enjoyed their lunch together and promised to keep in touch.

When Alan walked back to the office, he thought about change again. Without change the world and life would be very boring and predictable with no room for advancement. It's a natural process… like growing up. It happens with or without your consent.

Vivian hoped she hadn't come across as too aggressive in the interview. Detective Sharp was close to the age of her parents, and her family often disagreed with her on basic common beliefs. Besides being digitally illiterate, her parents were constantly talking about their physical ailments and memory lapses. When she brought up causes for real concern, like climate change and inflation, her parents reminded her that they were the generation to begin the "ecology" movement and address air pollution and had saved their money responsibly. Vivian didn't spend time trying to convince her parents to become better informed because she heard daily arguments from her own daughter about current trends she didn't quite understand.

Vivian grew up the youngest of three children. Her older siblings were already in high school when she was born and they wondered if their parents had lost their minds. But once they met Vivi, they loved her.

Vivi's Type A personality became her trademark, demonstrating her outgoing and determined ways. She excelled in everything she did, sports, school, and debate. She was innovative, outspoken and lively. Vivi loved debate and used logic and reasoning to understand a topic or a situation but was also known to be overly argumentative. This fact never bothered her. She graduated in the top 10% of her High School class. Her family was surprised when she announced her plans to join the police academy instead of law, but they never questioned her determination.

Vivi's early marriage and divorce had been a setback but raising her daughter provided a sense of purpose like no other. There were emotional and financial challenges, but Vivi was a strong woman who challenged norms and even tried to break barriers with her determination. She wanted this job in Boston.

TUESDAY, OCTOBER 3ʳᵈ

Alan walked outside his front door and stopped for a moment to appreciate the sun shining brilliantly on the remaining autumn leaves. The summer had been dry and hot with several storms passing through, and the outlook for winter was predicted to be cold once again. So, days like this were perfect. Alan felt for the phone in his pocket and wondered if he should take a photo and send it to Maggie. She would insist he stop for just a minute and do that exact thing. So he did and sent it to her.

He received an immediate reply. *'Alan! What a lovely photo!'* She added a sun and smiley face. He replied to her to have a great day and that he would call later.

Alan and Maggie had become close friends over the past few years. They had met when Alan was visiting his daughter in the Seattle area, and their friendship was instant. They appreciated how lucky they were to find each other. Maggie had recently been through a life changing event. Her daughter had taken a teaching position at UCONN, and so Maggie decided to sell her Bed and Breakfast business on an Island in the Pacific Northwest and move to the East Coast. Over the summer   she rented a condo in New Haven and was trying her best to adjust to unfamiliar surroundings. She missed her friends on the Island, but being close to her daughter was more important.

This also meant that Alan would see her more often. Another bonus was that the commute was now only two hours, so much easier than flying to the West Coast.

Alan once again reflected on change. He hadn't changed anything. He still lived in the same townhouse, had the same job, drove the same old car and even dressed in typical detective clothes. He looked down at his dark slacks, light blue button-down shirt, blue tie and comfortable shoes and wondered if he was due for some sort of makeover... a change. Do men his age do that? He should probably get out of his old and tired comfort zone and try to embrace new ideas.

On his way to work, Alan thought about all the tourists who flocked to New England to take in the autumn foliage. There seemed to be an overflow of visitors still hanging around the Boston area. The summer months were always crowded, and Alan and his station had been kept busy ensuring as much safety as possible. It was published in the media that burglary rates were steadily on the rise by five percent. Alan didn't like this sort of publicity and in fact, burglaries were on Alan's agenda for the station meeting he planned with his detectives that morning.

There had been a series of random attacks scattered over the past three months that were revealed to be the work of more than one suspect. At first, it was teenagers who committed home invasions while families were on vacations, and what worried Alan was the possibility of things getting out of control and becoming aggravated or ending up being an armed robbery. The law states that anyone who breaks into a home with the intent to commit a felony and is armed with a dangerous weapon to harm the occupant would be charged with a serious crime. And if these burglaries were committed by teens, and they were convicted, the sentence could be severe. Lately, though, Alan believed that gangs were involved making things even more dangerous.

Alan finally had to decide who he would hire for the detective slot. He considered the most senior applicant he interviewed because an officer with experience would make Alan's job easier. But was that the right approach? Hiring a younger person who understands the digital age demands might be the better decision. He then honestly considered his lack of technology skills. Did he feel anxious about being so illiterate about the high-tech world? What was he missing out on? He didn't want to start taking classes to find the conveniences offered in the tech world, especially when he had experts to call anyway. Alan depended on his tech team to handle the computer evidence and any other important information on a case. Was that enough? By the time Alan walked into the precinct, he still hadn't made up his mind who he would hire.

"Alan!" Lieutenant Johnson motioned for Alan to follow him into his office. He was a large man whose voice resounded throughout the unit and put everyone on notice. Alan was used to him and even amused sometimes when the older man shook his head and started in with his usual Monday morning quarterbacking. Or in this case, Monday night football.

"Did you see that game last night?" Johnson asked wearily.

Alan shook his head. "What was the score?"

"I turned it off after the third quarter. I think I'm

giving up on this Patriot team already. Sit down..." Alan sat in the comfortable wing back chair in front of the Lieutenant's desk. He always admired this office and considered it a class above other ones in the building. There were bookcases lining the walls and even a matching sofa. The abstract Persian rug gave an elegant feel to the room. Johnson seemed to clash with the decor.

Alan could see Johnson was irritated or worried and appeared to take a few slow deep breaths to calm himself. "Alan, there's something in the air that seems to be getting on my nerves. I'm worried that we have a much larger gang problem in the city than we know about. I'm talking about gangs who operate out of public housing developments... dealing drugs, targeting rivals in shootings, recruiting young people with enticements of appearing in songs and videos, and organized retail theft..."

Alan nodded. "My understanding is that they use force and intimidation, even violence, to take advantage of younger kids and turn them into a life of crime."

Johnson agreed. "I hate the thought of gangs using young kids to serve as lookouts and hold weapons and drug hauls... even engage in shootings. This is our new priority. Let's get busy on this right away." The Lieutenant stood to indicate the meeting was over. "By the way, who's your choice for the new detective?"

Alan surprised himself by saying, "I've decided to hire a young woman, Detective Vivian Collins. She appears to be a comparatively fresh alternative to our aging group. I think you'll appreciate her directness." Now that he had decided, Alan walked out of the office with renewed energy to focus on gangs... and burglaries.

The detectives were already seated in the conference room when Alan arrived for the morning meeting. He knew he was ten minutes late, but it couldn't be helped, and he didn't need an excuse. He walked to the front of the room and got right to the point. "Our concentration will be on burglaries this month, and the insurgence of gangs who are suspected of establishing their turf for retail theft and extortion."

Alan took a moment to consider why there were so many robberies in the Boston area. "I've heard every excuse for stealing, especially from young people... not having enough money, the store overcharges, or everyone's doing it. These transparent excuses have little bearing on the actual motivation to steal. For many it's a crime of opportunity. It's not necessarily about wanting the item but about taking advantage of the situation. I know in some cases, for example, a person has suffered an early attachment loss or trauma and may steal to compensate, but they can't fill an emotional hole by committing a crime."

Alan noticed a hand go up. He acknowledged the detective with a nod.

"Where do you want us to focus our investigations?"

"Good question. We all know about the gangs who operate out of public housing developments in the low-rent areas. They've been using force and intimidation to take advantage of the youngest sons and daughters living in these buildings and turn them into a life of crime. They teach these kids to steal, serve as lookouts and even hold the weapons in robberies. The young ones are enticed by being told they'll appear on media videos or in songs. We need to get them out of the gangs and into treatment, or, at least, back home."

Another hand went up. "Do you think we can use

Carla Tompkins' help identifying some vandals?" Everyone knew that Alan and Carla were good friends. Carla ran the teen center in the Back Bay and helped kids get into treatment and housing. She worked tirelessly for her clients and always appreciated the police involvement.

"Yes, of course. I'll be talking with Carla later today." Alan reached into his pocket for his notebook to remind him to call her. "And I'll have assignments posted today of stores and homes who have called to report burglaries. We need to reach out to all the businesses in the area and let them know this is a priority... to keep them safe." Alan nodded at his crew and then quickly left the room. He had no time for more questions.

When he reached his office, he rifled through his notes and sat down to call Detective Collins and offer her the job. He took a minute to be certain she would be the right fit by reviewing her references noting how people respected her honesty and flexibility. Alan believed that adaptability while working with a diverse team with differing ideas was a positive benefit to this job. He wasn't sure that Detective Collins would understand this at first. Why did he suspect that? Maybe he just needed to try and adapt to the unknown even in the face of uncertainty. In fact, he might just learn new things from this young detective. He made the call.

Vivian was having coffee with her sister, Anna, when she got the call. "This is Vivian Collins."

Alan was surprised by her directness. "Detective Collins, this is Detective Sharp. Do you have a minute?"

"Yes, sir." Vivian motioned to her sister that she was going outside the coffee shop to take the call.

"I'm offering you the job with my squad. Would you

like to accept?"

Vivian was stunned. She thought her chances to get the job were close to none. Not wasting a minute, she quickly answered, "Yes, sir. When do I start?"

Alan would arrange with HR to meet with Vivian the next day. He knew she had to move and get her daughter settled which meant he wouldn't see her in the office for at least a week.

Pleased with himself for finally deciding, Alan phoned Carla to see if he could take her to lunch.

"Nice to hear from you, Alan. How are you doing? We haven't heard a word from you in a couple weeks." Carla was speaking about herself and Sidney Miller, a Boston attorney who was one of Alan's favorite people, besides Carla. Sidney and Carla were trouble shooters, making headway in reshaping the city's response to teens in need of guidance. They spent hours writing proposals for better housing, mental evaluations, affordable drug rehab and counseling for kids in trouble. Being Black, they were better accepted by the poor communities who wanted someone on their side who understood their problems. Alan admired them greatly.

"Well, Carla, you know how it goes. I work, go home, and work some more. I've missed your company, too. How about lunch today?"

"Can I ask Sidney to come along?"

"Yes! Let's meet at the North Street Grille. My treat."

"Okay, how about 1:30? I've got a meeting that will take up my time until then."

"Sounds good. And we won't have the lunch crowd joining us."

A MATTER OF TIME

The North Street Grille was a friendly neighborhood spot with great food. Alan liked everything on the menu and often bought a loaf of their famous banana bread to take home. He arrived early and was surprised how crowded the place was for a Tuesday. He supposed it was the tourist crowd, still hanging around. He was lucky to get a seat by the window. He saw Sidney enter the restaurant and waved to him. As usual, his friend looked like he just stepped out of a magazine for eligible bachelors. He was wearing a well-cut suit and carrying his briefcase. Alan supposed he was going to court after their lunch.

Sidney waved back and walked quickly to the table. The men shook hands and then both looked quickly at their phones to see if Carla was on her way. "She said she had a meeting, so we'll just wait. Do you have a time schedule you're trying to meet?" Alan asked.

Sidney nodded. "I do, but it's not for a couple hours. I'm meeting a client at the courthouse. Anyway... how have you been my friend? We need to catch up."

Alan related news about Enrique's move, Maggie's settling into her new place, and hiring a new detective. "It's been a busy couple of weeks, as you can imagine. I just hope I made the right decision about who I hired."

"Why are you so doubtful?"

"She's young. I know we need this in the department, but I'll probably be challenged in some of my tried-and-true ways, I think. You know me... the same old person as always."

Sidney laughed just as Carla was walking in and greeting them. "Why are you laughing?" she asked Sidney after she gave him a quick kiss on the cheek.

"Alan thinks he's an old fogey. He just hired a young detective who's going to walk all over him."

Carla grinned at Alan. "Good for you. There may yet be hope for you to understand the tech world and maybe get to know how the new generation views us. When does she start?"

Alan related what he knew and then talked about how much he would miss Enrique. "You know how much I trusted him and how well we worked together. Now I've got to introduce this young woman to our department and sometime soon decide who will replace Enrique as my partner. Anyway, it's going to be a challenge."

The three friends ordered their meals and spoke candidly about their jobs and what they were doing socially. Maggie's name came up several times.

Carla then inquired, "Alan, you asked me to lunch with a purpose in mind. Care to tell me what that is?"

"We're investigating burglaries in and around your neighborhood and my detectives asked if you might give them some clues or guidance. Apparently, several burglaries involve teens who might be working with gangs. They're targeting younger kids to do some of the back-up work, and we're trying to identify the young ones and get them into programs."

"Do you want me to come in and speak to your group? Maybe I could answer questions at that time and then everyone will have the same information."

"Great idea! When are you free?"

Carla took out her phone to look at her calendar. "I could arrange an early time on Thursday if this works. Say, around 8:30."

Alan took out his notebook and wrote that down. "I'll arrange it."

Sidney shook his head. "You know, Alan, you have a calendar on your phone, too. Why don't you get Sam to help you set it up?"

Sam was Alan's twenty-four-year-old son who worked for Carla. She had hired him to do research and then sent him to take classes and work with teens who needed guidance. He was one of her valued employees.

Alan looked a bit sheepish. "He's tried. I'm just so used to my notebook. Old dog... old tricks..."

When lunch ended, they promised to meet again. Alan hurried back to the precinct to put Carla on the Thursday schedule. He wanted the unit to have their questions ready for her.

WEDNESDAY, OCTOBER 4th

Vivian hardly slept. After getting the phone call from Detective Sharp saying she got the job, she returned to join her sister in the restaurant and started to plan her next move. Anna and her husband had a large home and were pleased to offer their basement for as long as Vivi needed it. "Our kids are grown! We're going to love having you live with us as long as you want." Anna was ten years older than Vivian and always acted as a mother. She was a tenth grade English teacher and her husband, Steve, was a pilot. They had managed their busy household with two active children in a way that made it look easy.

Vivian knew she needed all the help she could get with her daughter who was more than reluctant to move to a new city. When she told Sadie about the job the night before, she heard the anger in her responses. Sadie carried on in her loud and demeaning voice that she didn't want to move and refused to leave her friends. But that was exactly why a move was called for. Sadie had been in trouble with her so-called buddies and consequently had been suspended from school. Vivian had her doing online classes but actually wanted a totally new environment for Sadie. Plus, Sadie looked up to her Aunt Anna because she was calm and a good listener. It might be better than therapy for Sadie.

A MATTER OF TIME

Anna and Steve's basement was more like a second home. There was a full kitchen, an open living space and three bedrooms. Vivian would use the extra bedroom as an office and give Sadie the larger bedroom. There was even a separate entrance to the downstairs which would give them more privacy. Maybe Vivian would let Sadie have a cat, if Anna agreed to it. That might soothe her defensive daughter's attitude and give her something to care about.

Vivian was on her way this morning to speak with HR and get the paperwork started. She had already given her notice to the Hartford station when she began her search for a new job. Hopefully, they would accept her decision to leave by the following week.

Alan overslept. He never did that! It was already 7:30 and by now he should have been on his way to the office. If things were normal, he would call Enrique and let him handle things until he arrived. Another adjustment.

He was feeling out of sorts by the time he got to the precinct fifty minutes later. As he sat down to review his schedule, one of his lead detectives knocked on the door. "There's been a shooting."

"Where?"

"Roxbury... and it looks like gangs. Do you want me to take it or will you?"

"I'll go and let you know if I need backup."

Roxbury was one of the oldest communities in the state, home to a diverse community of Black, Hispanic, and Asian families and was now becoming popular with young professionals. There were safe neighborhoods in the district, but around seven percent were known to be dangerous, and those were generally the northwest neighborhoods where a crime was committed about every three and a half hours. Crimes were most often reported in retail areas where few people live, but everyone knew ultimately that crime happens in parks, schools, factory areas and airports, too. Alan was on his way to West Roxbury.

The detective reported that four people were involved in the shooting and one person was dead. When Alan arrived at the scene, a large police presence was already controlling the area where several citizens had gathered. Boston Emergency Medical Services had quickly responded, and three victims had been rushed to the hospital. Alan approached the lead patrolman to learn about the crime.

Reading from his notes the patrolman highlighted the details. "The victim is a fifteen-year-old boy who was apparently shot in his back. A person driving by saw the boy fall and stopped to help. He then saw three other victims further down the street who were hurt, but still conscious. He called 911."

"Where is the witness?"

"He's standing by the emergency vehicle. His name is Charles Durham."

Alan walked over to Mr. Durham and nodded. "I understand you stopped to help, sir, and we're very appreciative. I'm Detective Sharp and I'd like to ask you a few questions."

Alan saw that Charles was young, probably in his mid to late twenties. He appeared very shaken up. "Did you see anyone running away from the scene?"

Charles shook his head repeatedly. "No, which is strange because I saw that kid fall. Whoever did it must have been hidden, or the kid was trying to get away after being shot. It's all so horrible!" Charles held his head in his hands.

"From what location was he running? East? West?"

"He was running East and then he fell. Is he dead?"

"Yes, I'm afraid so. Would you mind coming to the station and giving a statement? It shouldn't take long and then you can be on your way."

Charles agreed and insisted on driving himself there. Alan nodded to a young policeman standing by and asked him to follow Charles to the station.

Lloyd Randel, the longtime medical examiner for the Boston station, was arriving as Alan turned to view the scene. He and Lloyd had been through many homicides and never got used to seeing a victim. This time was even worse because it was a child. Alan acknowledged his friend, "Lloyd... thanks for getting here so quickly."

Lloyd shook his head to indicate his reluctance having to deal with another death. Both men approached the victim and saw it was a Hispanic boy, dressed in blue jeans, a green hooded sweatshirt, and what looked like expensive running shoes. He was lying face down on the ground with his arms stretched over his head as if to skid onto the pavement. Lloyd knelt beside the body and looked like he was saying a prayer. He then turned the boy over and began his investigation.

Alan looked around to find more information on the victim. He once again found the lead patrolman and asked if he found any ID on the boy.

"Carlos Rivera, age fifteen, lives on Coleman Street and has been suspended from school for truancy."

"It's only October!" Alan said. "He barely had time to skip school!"

"Do you want his house address? Are you going to speak with his family?"

"Yes. I'll go now. Is there anything about the other three kids?"

"All of them have stab wounds, but not critical. Do you want me to go talk with them?"

Alan once again felt at a loss without Enrique. He would have trusted him to follow up on the three others. "Thanks, but I'll have one of my detectives talk with them." He called the station and asked for Sasha Lane. She had just passed her detective exam and was waiting for the paperwork to be completed. But for all purposes, she was officially a detective.

"Detective Lane, I need you to go to the hospital and interview three teens who have just been brought in with stab wounds. I have little information so far, but it happened in West Roxbury. I'm with the homicide victim and on my way to talk with the family. After that, I'll join you at the hospital."

Sasha wrote down the information as she put on her jacket. She no longer wore a patrol uniform and was dressed in a black pants suit with a cream-colored blouse. She had the detective badge on her belt and was still trying to get used to wearing it.

Boston Medical Center was in the South End neighborhood and had the reputation of being indispensable because it cared for people who were underserved and many without a health plan. Everyone who walked through the door was treated with compassion and provided with excellent care. When Sasha arrived at the hospital, she was escorted to the emergency area where the three boys were located. A patrol officer was on duty and nodded when Sasha showed her badge. "What can you tell me?" she asked.

The officer shook his head. "Not much. The ambulance dropped the boys off an hour ago and we're waiting to hear from their families. The doctor in charge treated their superficial wounds and then left. So far, only PA's have been in to talk with them. They seemed shaken up and worried about the other boy."

"Do they know the details?"

"No. Are you going to tell them?"

"I'll wait until Detective Sharp gets here. He's talking with the victim's family now."

Alan hated this part of his job. He parked in front of a modest one-story home on an older established street about four miles from the crime scene. The median household income in Roxbury was around $45,000-$50,000 and, even so, families probably had two salaries to afford to live there. He looked at his watch, it was already 11:00. Getting out of his car, he saw another vehicle speed down the street and park haphazardly near his car. An anxious appearing hispanic woman exited the car and ran frantically towards the Rivera house while wrestling her purse for keys. Alan stood and watched as she entered, leaving the door ajar. All he could think was that Carlos' mother had heard. Her son had been shot.

Knocking gently on the open door, Alan waited. Hearing a distant voice, he called out, "Hello. May I come in? I'm Detective Sharp."

The woman walked tentatively from the other room, holding on to the wall for support. She was petite and seemed childlike as she collapsed onto the floor. "Please don't tell me it's true..."

Alan helped her get up and walked her to a living room area and settled her on to the sofa. "Mrs. Rivera? Can I call anyone for you?" he asked.

The woman shook her head and sobbed. "What happened?" she whispered.

"I'm so sorry to tell you that your son, Carlos, was killed on a street in West Roxbury today. Carlos and his friends were attacked and appeared to be running from their assailants. Please let me call someone for you."

The woman reached for her phone and handed it to Alan. "His father is Edgar Rivera. His number's on my contact list."

Alan called the number as he walked to the kitchen to get Mrs. Rivera a glass of water. The kitchen was tidy with pictures of Carlos and two other children on the walls. It appeared to be a gallery of school photos lined up in order of classes. Alan felt his heart ache.

"Hello... Mona? Why are you calling me at work?" an angry voice answered the phone call.

"Mr. Rivera, this is Detective Sharp from the Boston Police, and I would like you to come home now."

"Why? What's this about?"

"It's about your son Carlos, sir. I need to talk with you."

Alan heard an abrupt click and hoped the man was on his way. Dealing with grieving parents was difficult and he needed backup. He called the station. "Can you send a nearby officer to this address? Let them know it's important to come right away."

Ten minutes later a police car drove up and Officer John Rosen walked quickly to the house. Alan informed Rosen of the situation and introduced him to Mrs. Rivera. He appreciated that Rosen, an older officer, immediately sat beside the grieving woman and offered his sympathy.

Five minutes later an angry man stormed into the house. "What is this all about? What did Carlos do now?" The man was short in stature, but thick in build. He was wearing a mechanics type overall and still had grease on his hands.

Alan introduced himself and led him into the living room. When Edgar saw his wife crying, he walked over and laid his hands on her shoulder. "Mona, what happened?"

"Oh Edgar, Carlos... *El esta muerto...*" and her sobs continued.

Edgar sat heavily beside her. "What do you mean?"

Officer Rosen spoke in quiet Spanish. "*Lamento mucho su peridida.*" Alan stood by, watching the grieving parents in silence, with a slight bow to his head.

Finally, he sat down on a nearby chair. "Mr. and Mrs. Rivera, I'm very sorry for your loss. Unfortunately, I must ask you some questions about Carlos before I can leave." He paused to be certain they understood. "When was the last time you spoke with your son?"

Edgar looked up at Alan with a blank expression. "Today... this morning." He looked at his wife. "We were all getting ready to leave. How did this happen? What happened?"

Alan explained what he knew so far, including the other three boys' involvement. "Do you know who these boys are?"

Edgar and Mona both shook their heads. Edgar spoke solemnly. "He has lots of friends. Some are not so good though and we have told him to quit hanging out with those kids." Edgar looked away and tried to compose himself. He wanted to be strong for his wife who was now leaning into his shoulder.

"And how about your other children? I saw the photos in the kitchen." Alan didn't want Carlos's sisters to hear what happened from someone other than their parents. He also wanted to ensure they were safe. "Can you call the schools and have them wait to be picked up?"

Without questioning this, Edgar reached for his phone and made the call. "I must go get them."

Alan agreed and asked Officer Rosen to go along for support and because he spoke Spanish, he could listen for anything of importance. When they left, Alan asked Mona to let him see Carlos' bedroom. As they walked down the hall, Alan noticed three bedrooms, one appeared to have a neat and functional layout for the parents, another looked like a colorful girl's room and last was a small room in the back that belonged to Carlos. A double bed took up most of the space with a bookcase on a facing wall. Alan walked over to the bookcase and saw a switchblade on the shelf. He turned and looked at Mona, "Does this belong to Carlos?" He pointed at the knife.

Mona shook her head, "No... no! We refuse to have him carry a knife. We tell him it could be used against him." She began to suddenly shake, and so Alan led her to the bed and asked her to sit down. "I'm going to have to take this."

"Does Carlos belong to a gang?" Alan was beginning to suspect that the boys' parents were unaware of the trouble their son may have been in.

Mona shook her head. "He's a good boy."

"Did you know he hasn't been in school? We have a report of his truancy."

Mona's posture stiffened suddenly. "He told us he was back in school when we got a phone call from the principal. You mean he wasn't going?"

"Mrs. Rivera, Carlos was found miles from school with his friends. They all skipped going to class. We need to find out what they were doing."

Alan's phone rang. "Detective Sharp."

It was Detective Lane. "The boys will be released in a few hours. They have superficial wounds and have been treated. So far, I've only spoken to one of them. He seems to be the leader and advised the other two to keep quiet. When will you be here?"

Alan noted the frustration in her voice. He knew he had promised to follow up with the questioning and now had to decide what his next step was. "Go ahead and do an informal interview with all three boys. We need as much information as possible before the families decide to stop them from talking. I'll be there as soon as I can."

Rivera's front door slammed open and two young girls came running down the hall until they found their mother. Both girls were crying. "What happened to Carlos? Where is he?" The oldest girl was demanding to know while glaring at Alan. He guessed she was around ten or eleven. It was hard to tell.

"I'm Detective Sharp, and what's your name?"

Still glaring, she responded, "Amaya... and my sister is Sara."

"I'm going to let you talk with your mother while I go

and speak with the other officer." Alan walked slowly out of the room after nodding to Mona. He knew she would have to comfort her daughters and gently tell them what she knew. He glanced back at her sadly, and then quietly closed the door.

Officer Rosen and Edgar were waiting in the hallway, speaking in Spanish about the changes in the neighborhood.

Alan once again appreciated this officer. He pulled him aside for a moment to say, "Officer, I need to go and interview the other boys at the hospital. Can you stay with the family until I can get another detective here to help the Rivera's deal with this tragedy?"

"Of course. I can stay as long as they need me."

Alan looked at his watch. It was already 1:30. The day was swiftly passing, and he didn't have a handle on one thing.

Officer Lane had the three boys in a conference room at the hospital. Their parents had been called, but so far, not one of them had shown up. The boys didn't seem to care but still wanted to be released. When Alan arrived, Sasha had only gotten as far as their names, phone numbers, and addresses. She had called the information into the station and was waiting to hear if any one of them had a record.

Alan sat down at the head of the table and looked at each boy. "Look here," he demanded with a heavy sigh, "your friend Carlos is dead. I want you to tell me who did this." He wasn't going to play games with these kids. He needed answers.

The boys just stared back at him, refusing to say anything. "Well, then, I'm taking you down to the station to get a formal interview. In the meantime, I'll be talking with the officers at the scene and find out what part you played in this crime. We have witnesses and are looking at any CCTV in the area. Let's go."

Alan stood and nodded to Officer Lane. "You can take one and I'll take the other two."

It was going to be a long day.

THURSDAY, OCTOBER 5th

Carla entered the station to offer support. She had heard about the shooting and knew her scheduled talk with the unit might be canceled. If this was gang related, she would feel the tension and right now she only offered alternatives to help get kids out of trouble. The officers wanted answers now, not solutions. She walked into Alan's office and sat in the chair next to his desk. "Should I do this another day?"

Alan shook his head. "We have gang problems every day. I still need you to give current perspectives on what we can do to help kids stay away from these controlling gangs. I'm not saying that this was a gang hit, but when I spoke to the other three kids involved yesterday, they were frightened and didn't tell us anything for fear of being targeted."

Alan had spent hours speaking to the three boys. They seemed tough at first but eventually broke down and told him they couldn't say anything because the gang leaders in charge would go after their families.

Carla nodded. "It's a common excuse. But what I find out a lot of times is that when kids get into trouble repeatedly, the families don't even care one way or another. They've lost contact and don't want to deal with their kids anyway. That's when kids join gangs."

Alan leaned forward. "But the kid who was shot was from a very caring family. As far as they were concerned, he was attending school and doing okay. They didn't know about these friends or any gang affiliation."

"So, do you think he was at the wrong place and was caught…?"

"It appears that might be the case. The three boys said they barely knew him."

"You know, Alan, sometimes that's what I find with these gangs. They groom kids with all sorts of promises to get them to join. If this kid was on the younger side, he may have been targeted just for the purpose of using him to get by the police. Who would suspect a good kid?"

They both sat and thought about that.

Gangs have always been a problem in big cities and even small towns. Their street presence usually amounted to three or more members ages twelve through twenty-four. Generally, gang members shared a tribal identity, typically linked to a name or symbol so they could be recognized by other gangs. Group identity was the most important thing to the members, and they wore it proudly. Youth were easily attracted by this but pulled into gangs for several other reasons: the attraction of increased reputation and social status, the desire to be with friends or family already in gangs, or the promise of money, drugs, excitement, cultural pride and sometimes it offered protection. On the other hand, besides victimization, gang members often risked dropping out of school, early parenthood or lack of stable employment.

Carla dealt with these issues every day. Her teen center was filled with kids who were in trouble with drugs associated with gang activity. She often thought that gang membership was part of their drug addiction, providing an ego booster that led to aggressive behavior. More of a problem was the increased interest in carrying guns. Carla worried and would never be able to keep pace with all the growing addictions nor have enough resources in place to help fight them.

Alan spoke first. "I still need to gather my detectives together and have you review any options you can offer." Looking at his watch, he said, "I'll take you to the conference room to set up."

Several detectives were already gathered in the room. Weekly meetings were important, and Alan was aware of their busy schedules and made the meetings as short and concise as possible. Carla waved to several of them and put on a microphone so her voice would carry, and she didn't have to repeat her message over again.

At exactly 9:00 Alan walked to the front of the room and introduced Carla. "Listen up... we need to hear about the ongoing gang movement in our city and what resources we can use to decrease involvement with young people." He stepped aside and let Carla begin.

"The other day I had a twelve-year-old boy come into my center all beat up. He said he had been attacked by a gang... one kid had pinned down his arms and legs and sat on his chest. He was told to keep out of the area... their turf... unless he wanted to be killed. Thank goodness he was released. So why was he there? Why him? How can we let young kids know where they can be safe? We've got to develop new strategies." She paused and looked around the room. "It's not always about the programs we can offer; it's got to be involving the parents and communities who set the tone for these kids. We know kids need someplace to go, things to do, so they have choices besides joining up with gangs. I believe there should be ongoing workshops to inform families of strategies for preventative measures, conflict resolution and peer engagement. If we can motivate kids to look inward, envision and actualize a better lifestyle they might avoid being involved in a gang."

A voice interrupted Carla. "Who are the kids we're talking about?"

"Good question. First, we know individuals of color are at most risk. Next are at-risk or proven risk young people... those who are less likely to transition successfully into adulthood. You know the signs, trouble in school, arguing and threatening to run away, shoplifting, being in the wrong crowd, losing their cool, lying, drugs and alcohol, lack of confidence..."

One voice yelled out, "That sounds like my teenagers! Well... not the drugs and alcohol I hope... but aren't all teens going through some of this?"

Carla nodded her head. "Of course. But how many are going to decide to belong to a gang as a means of self-esteem or to boost their confidence? What I'm suggesting is we want to help parents cope with their teens by giving them support. Setting up classes and asking for mentors to be available is a good beginning."

Carla went on to point out the programs that were already in place. She also asked for volunteers in her teen center.

Alan knew his detectives were on board and looking for answers. He stepped forward and gave the report on the boy who was killed and the other three victims. "It appears from his phone contacts that Carlos might have been lured into the area by the promise of starring in a commercial. He was a very good-looking kid, and we found out that he dreamed of acting on the big screen. He had skipped school a few times and, so far, we don't know what he was doing on the days he skipped, but we're speaking with his friends later today. The other three boys have a history and have been caught for shoplifting and destruction of property. Their stab wounds were minor, but they refused to say who had come after them. They each had a tattoo of a ring on their left middle finger. We believe this means they might belong to a gang, although we can't identify which one."

Alan took out his notebook to check on a detail. "So far, the three boys' families have not made contact. We suspect that the boys are on the run or homeless. We had no reason to keep them here and so I want you to keep an eye out for them. I have alerted all patrol officers to do the same." Alan nodded at the group, and then escorted Carla out the door, thanking her for all her ideas.

Edgar Rivera was waiting by Alan's office when he returned. "Mr. Rivera, how can I help you?"

Edgar was filled with anger and in a state of grief so obvious that Alan hurried him into the office and shut the door. "Please sit down and let's talk."

Edgar sat heavily onto the chair and put his hands to his face. When he looked up his eyes were filled with tears. "I want someone to pay for what happened to my boy. He was a good boy... never caused any trouble... always happy... someone must suffer for what they did to him." Tears began to roll down his face as he drew slow and steady breaths.

Alan nodded. "Mr. Rivera, we will do everything in our

power to find out who did this and punish them. I promise you that. I just met with my detectives instructing them to do just that. How can I help you and your family at this time?"

Edgar stared at Alan and asked, "When can we have my son's body so we can bury him?"

Alan knew that was probably the reason why he had come to the station. Most parents wanted the opportunity to immediately mourn and grieve with family and close friends. It's a parent's nightmare to lose a child and the Rivera's would need a lot of support. "I'll let you know when the time comes. We're still investigating the circumstances." Alan didn't want to say too much. He knew an autopsy had been ordered and the body would have to stay in custody for a while.

Edgar nodded but still pushed. "I need my son's body soon. We need to prepare a wake and burial." He stood up. "You understand, Detective Sharp, that our anger is deep. We have ways to see results."

Was that a threat? Alan watched the man leave the office and tried to deal with what the man insinuated. Once again, he missed Enrique. They could have talked this over and decided what steps to take. Instead, he called Detective Lane.

Sasha was writing up her report when she got the phone call. She had noticed an angry man leaving Alan's office and wondered if this involved the young boy who had been killed. Alan motioned her in when he saw her at his door.

"Carlos Rivera's father was just in, and from everything he said, I believe he might want to take revenge on the person who shot his son. I know it's understandable, but we should investigate his background and know if we should be worried."

Sasha nodded. "Do you want me to do a background

check and also keep a watch on him?"

Alan nodded. "That's exactly what I want you to do. And then get back to me if anything comes up that looks suspicious. I know the man is in pain, but I don't want him to make his life worse by doing something crazy."

When Sasha left his office, Alan considered her as a replacement for Enrique. She was dedicated, professional and seemed adaptable to finding solutions without escalating the situations. Being a Black woman, Sasha was respected for her calm and peaceful interactions with the diverse public population along with finding a balance in a male-dominated field.

Just then, Lieutenant Johnson called from his office. "Do you have a minute?"

Reluctantly, but to himself, Alan grimaced. "I'll be there in a minute."

Five minutes later, Alan sat in the comfortable wingback chair in front of the Lieutenant's desk. Trying to keep the tension out of his voice, Alan asked, "What do you need?"

"There's been a break-in reported at a residence in the Beacon Hill area. The family is wealthy and both parents' work. The father is an attorney, and the mother is an investment counselor. They have three teenage kids. It doesn't seem to be the usual grab and go variety because nothing of value is missing."

"What was the damage?"

"Well. That's the thing... the place was tossed as if they were searching for something, which makes me think it might be a game of some kind to see how much fear they could provoke."

"Okay, but why is this a priority? I've got my team focused on several burglaries and we can add this to our list, but things are tight right now because of the murder in Roxbury and I'm also training a new detective."

"Alan, this is personal. The wife in this case is my sister-in-law... my wife's youngest sister. I promised I'd discretely handle this because they don't want any media attention. The husband is thinking about running for attorney general soon. If there's a hint of a scandal of some sort, which they say there isn't, they just don't want any bad press. I want you to follow up on this and see what you think."

Alan knew that any negative social media, whether it's true or not, confirmed or not, could damage a reputation or might totally ruin it, especially if you're on the public watch list. Running for office would be a good example of wanting to stay clear of anything negative.

Alan nodded his agreement to take the case. "Send me the address and report and I'll get on it." He hoped to assign this to another detective and get back to the Rivera investigation.

Alan was frustrated with how fast the morning had slipped past. He needed to spend time reviewing the comments from the interviews with the three boys last night. The oldest one, Jet, had nothing to say. He just kept shaking his head when asked a question. From the police reports, he had been picked up for disturbance and retail theft twice before. When asked about this, he just stared and shook his head. The second kid, Damon, seemed more outgoing. He told Alan he had recently been mugged, and his ID had been stolen along with his phone. The report on him was burglary and truancy. The youngest of the three kids, RJ, appeared to be shaken up. He darted his eyes between the other two kids and said he didn't know what had happened. The boys were all wearing similar sweatshirts and expensive running shoes. They all had tattoo rings on their left hands. If not affiliated with a gang, they appeared to wear a message of belonging or wanting to belong. There was only so much Alan knew he could do for them. Because no one had come to pick them up, he had called a social worker.

Alan had called ahead that morning and made a one o'clock appointment to meet with the Principal at Carlos' school. Gathering information about the boys' movements along with names of his friends, would give Alan something to start the investigation. So far, there was nothing his family could say, except that Carlos went to school. He didn't play sports or have any other outside commitments. He liked to play video games, they admitted. *Maybe this was true of a lot of teens these days,* Alan thought. They all seemed to be wrapped up with video games.

Principal Lauder met Alan promptly and invited him into his office. "I'm very sad about what's happened. Carlos was a good kid. I imagine his family is going crazy trying to figure this out."

Alan raised his eyebrows. "Figure what out?"

Lauder looked surprised, "Carlos being killed. I can't imagine their grief."

Alan nodded and quietly asked, "Do you think that Carlos had enemies at the school? Anyone who was bullying him or held a grudge of some sort?"

Lauder asked Alan to take a seat by his desk and then pulled out a file and opened it. "Carlos was not attending school regularly. We had been in touch with his family, and they were surprised, but promised they would get him here. This past week he was absent two days and late one day. I was going to contact the family tomorrow... the end of the week... and see what the problem was."

"Do you usually contact families... even if the student might be ill?"

"Carlos has been truant already this year, Detective. He's on my radar to watch and encourage better decisions. He was always a very good kid and lately seemed to be making some poor choices... especially this year."

"Who does Carlos hang around with? Anyone in particular?"

"He was a quiet boy. I know he had a couple of friends in elementary school, but they attend a different school now. Last year he hung around with a couple of kids, but this year they seemed to have lost interest. I really can't give you the name of anybody who might know Carlos well enough to have a clue about what's happened."

Alan looked around the office. It was sparse, with very few personal items displayed. "How long have you been here?"

Lauder looked at Alan and shook his head. "I'm only the interim Principal. I took over last Spring and the school district has found a permanent position for me. I'll be leaving in a few months."

"So, you don't know the students as well as, say, the former Principal might have. Where is that person?"

"Tina Norton, she's on maternity leave. In fact, I think she's planning on returning after the holidays."

Alan asked for her name and number. He knew that school districts were always in need of qualified administrators, and he imagined this school had probably more turnover because of being in the vicinity of poor families. Plus, the classes were large, and the students might need more guidance than the staff could possibly handle. He gave Lauder his card and said he would get back with him.

When Alan got in his car he phoned Tina Norton. He left a message and hoped she would return his call soon.

Where should he go from here? He had picked up Carlos's computer when he went through his room and hoped the tech people might find something to point him in another direction. Alan also wanted to find more out about the gang affiliation the other three boys belonged to. If they all had the same tattoo, it meant something.

He had missed lunch, so he stopped at a deli to get his usual salad on his way back to the station. He always bought a Cobb salad, but today he decided on the chicken Caesar. Maybe if he stepped out of his usual habits, he might be encouraged to see things differently. He smiled at the thought... he read that a single detour from a usual habit could help change one's behavior. Maybe he was just kidding himself and grasping for a way to handle all the changes he saw evolving these days.

Sasha was waiting for Alan when he returned to the station. She referred to the notes on her phone to update Alan about the three boys. "A social worker came to talk with the boys. She had been in touch with Jet and Damon's family, and so they were sent home with the admonishment to stay there. RJ, however, is still waiting and will not be released until someone takes responsibility for him."

"But they have an address, right?"

Sasha nodded. "The social worker said if no one shows

up, she'd have to drive him to his house and talk to the person in charge. She doesn't seem too hopeful."

"Why's that?"

"The address is in a bad area and some of the houses are condemned. She thinks RJ is living on the street and doesn't want to say anything. He's only 16 and so she'll have to find him a bed if that's the case."

"Poor kid. Let me know what happens. And Sasha, I'd like you to fill in for Detective Mendez's position for a while. I need someone to work closely with me, and I believe you're my best choice."

Sasha was pleased, but also skeptical. She admired Detective Sharp and yet knew his relationship with Enrique had lasted years and they could almost read each other with a glance. She couldn't imagine even approaching him with a new idea or questioning his way of thinking. "Thank you, sir. I'll do my best."

"And, Sasha, we have a new detective joining our squad and I'd like her to follow you around for a couple weeks. She starts on Monday."

Sasha had already heard about Vivian Collins. Having another woman on the force was always good news. She also liked that Vivian was older and not as young as some of the other detectives who had joined over the years. Hopefully, they would have a lot in common.

"Sir, where would you like me to begin on this case?"

Alan raised his eyebrows and smiled. "I don't suppose you might call me Alan?"

Sasha shook her head. "I'll try, but it won't be easy."

Alan nodded. "I'd like you to follow up with CCTV surveillance in the area where Carlos was shot and speak with anyone in the vicinity about the shooting. I'm also curious to find out more about those tattoo rings the three kids had." Before Shasha turned to go, Alan drew in a long breath, "We've already let too much time go by and need to get on top of this now."

Sasha agreed. "I'll report back as soon as I find something."

Alan finished his salad and phoned down to the tech center. "Did you find anything of interest on the computer I sent you? It belonged to Carlos Rivera."

"Yeah... something interesting. It looks like he was messing around with a strange social site. There's a chatroom that's known for cyberbullying and scammers that his parents would have blocked if they knew. It's a grooming site that focuses on self-esteem and self-image. But the real thing they do is groom the kid for pornography."

Alan shook his head. "I understand that Carlos was a handsome kid and could be enticed with offers of exposure to see his image out there. Send me the link and anything else you've found that will help my investigation."

Alan thought about another case he had with a young girl who wanted to be a star. She had even enrolled in a modeling school that encouraged her to seek a future of glamour. She was kidnapped and a target to be trafficked when they located her and the criminals. He thought about all the schemes that lured kids these days with games or lies that promised money and fame. How can parents keep up with the criminals, the apps, and the insidious promises?

The day was getting away from Alan. He was tired and felt an ache in his back. When was his last doctor appointment? When he opened his computer to check, he found the police report the Lieutenant sent him about the Beacon Hill burglary. He walked over to the comfortable sofa Maggie had insisted he buy for his office and settled in. If this was to be a priority, he needed time to digest the case and make notes on how to proceed.

Once he scanned the report, Alan decided to call the Murphys' home number in hopes of leaving a message. "Hello, this is the Murphy residence," a young voice said.

Alan took a second to respond. "This is Detective Sharp from the Boston precinct, is your mother or father available?"

"I'm sorry, but they're still at work. Do you want their numbers?"

"No, not necessary. Will you please tell them I called. This is in reference to the burglary you had at your house. I'm following up."

"Okay. I'll tell them." And then there was a click. Alan laid the report down on his desk. It would have to wait.

FRIDAY, OCTOBER 6th

Vivian had spent the week moving into her sister's basement, talking with HR and trying to convince her daughter that the move would be positive for them both. Listening to Sadie rant on and on about missing her friends and hating Boston, Vivian tried to appear nonjudgemental and promised to make things work. She knew Sadie didn't want to admit she had been bullied, drained of her dignity, and ostracized in her school. Vivian just wanted her to learn that there comes a time in life when you walk away from the drama and people who make you feel inadequate.

Vivian was aware that her personality often clashed with Sadie's. Sadie had always been a sweet child who had friends and relatives who adored her. The teen years were typical of the attitude she had now, and Vivian knew it would pass. Instead of engaging in further arguments, Vivian was trying to pick her battles wisely.

Vivian had her own faults. She knew she was opinionated and outspoken to a fault, and it sometimes took physical and mental exhaustion to stop the inner chatter for fear that things might fall apart from inattention. She needed to focus more on observation, not judging, and try to see how the people around her were communicating both verbally and nonverbally. Hopefully, Detective Sharp will give her time to develop new ways of responding and modify her behavior. She needed to change.

Sasha wanted to speak with Alan first. She met him at the door and followed him into his office. "I have some CCTV information on the surrounding areas of the murder." She sat on the chair next to Alan's desk and pulled out her laptop. "It looks like a group of older teens were chasing the three boys into the park. They were all wearing hoodies and were probably aware of the cameras. I lost track of them when they reached the neighborhood street. As you can see, the hooded teens have weapons... three had knives, and the tallest one had a pistol. My guess is that they didn't mean to kill the boys, but Carlos probably got too far away, and things got out of hand."

"Why do you think this?"

"This is gang territory, sir. These teens were probably foot soldiers who protected their territory and regularly ran people off who might threaten their community."

"Community?"

"Well, there's a project close by that seems to be a city within a city. It's known to invite teens who are involved with vandalism and shoplifting. A number of the tenants are drug addicts, have done some street hustling and jail time, and many are homeless. It's a refuge for some people."

"What about the tattoos on the fingers? Any relation to the project?"

"Not that I found. Ring finger tattoos have become increasingly popular because a few celebrities have jumped on the trend. I guess some teens are doing this as a personal way to symbolize a strong commitment for someone. But so far, I haven't associated this with a gang."

"Okay, let's put this aside for the moment. I have a meeting this morning with the former principal of Carlos' school. She's taking a maternity leave but knew Carlos from last year. I'd like you to come with me."

An hour later, Sasha and Alan were on their way to Dorchester, where Tina Norton lived. The character of the homes along the way changed from mostly double-wide mobile homes to individually constructed one level ranch style brick homes. They finally drove up to a classic farmhouse with an inviting wraparound porch.

Tina was expecting the police and had just put the baby down for a nap. She was lucky that her little one was so flexible and good natured. When she opened the door, she put her finger to her mouth to indicate quiet, just in case the baby decided to stir.

Alan smiled and quietly introduced himself and Sasha. They were led into a homey kitchen with the smell of coffee filling the space. "Can I offer you a cup of coffee? It's decaf." Sasha nodded, but Alan declined.

"Mrs. Norton, we only have a few questions. You've heard about the attack on Carlos Rivera, and we'd like your input on how he did in school. Who were his friends... did he have enemies... get bullied."

Tina set a mug in front of Sasha and offered cream and sugar. Sasha shook her head, and they watched Tina add sugar to her cup. "I am so sad about Carlos dying. He was a good kid. Last year as a freshman, he had a difficult time making the transition into high school and I think it was because he was younger than most students. He had a late summer birthday, and he was still growing, appearing much younger. His teachers were worried about his ability to keep up with the work."

Alan repeated his question, "What about the other students? Did they accept him?"

Tina thought for a moment. "Detective, younger students dress and talk like all the others, mimic their behavior and overextend themselves trying to gain approval. My theory is that while social integration matters, self-worth should not be tied to approval from others. Many students do turn to reckless rebellion in hopes of being viewed as mature, but I didn't see this behavior in Carlos."

Alan nodded. "Tell me which students were friends with Carlos."

Tina pulled out a folder from a pile on the counter. "I asked for my file on Carlos to be emailed. His teachers said he had a few friends, but he tended to seek out the attention of older students. I believe their connection was through video games, which is very common especially for boys. This becomes their social avenue."

Alan wrote this down. He would ask the Rivera's about Carlos' video access. "Can you give me any names?"

"I would prefer not to. I've been on leave since last spring and haven't been involved with my students. But I will give you the name of a concerned teacher, Amos Philips. He was Carlos' homeroom teacher, and he would know more than I do."

Alan looked at Sasha to see if she had a question. "Mrs. Norton, do you think that Carlos was bullied?"

Tina shook her head. "No. But he was a good-looking boy, and he may have been pushed around to make him tough. Sometimes kids do this to one another... it's kind of a protection."

"Were his parents involved with his education?"

"My understanding was that both parents worked, and Carlos had to take care of his sisters when they got home from school."

Sasha continued. "Have you ever met the Riveras?"

"Yes, during parents' night."

"And what was your impression?"

Tina looked down at her coffee cup and shook her head slightly. "I hate to say anything negative, but Mr. Rivera seemed to be the dominant figure in the family. He seemed to have a deeply rooted mistrust of the school, and we were trying our best to learn what his biggest fear was about our community. It was becoming tiresome. Whatever we did, we could do nothing to help him understand our system."

Sasha nodded, because she understood the problem on a personal level. Her mother had been a teacher and always found it difficult to placate, persuade or convince parents that she was on their side and only had the best intentions for their child. "What was Carlos' reaction to his father's behavior?" Sasha asked.

"I really can't say. He never talked about his home life, as far as I know."

The detectives thanked Tina for her time and drove back to the precinct. Alan had been impressed with Sasha's inquiries and thought he had made a good decision to have her work with him.

"I like your questions about the family, Sasha. Let's pursue this in case Mr. Rivera intends to seek revenge and go after the person who killed his son. He has a temper, and I understand his grief, but he may end up in jail if he takes things too far."

"I'll stop by this afternoon and check in with Mrs. Rivera."

"Good. Report back to me later. I'm going to pay a visit to the project in Roxbury where these teens may live. Send me the CCTV coverage you have, and I'll take it with me."

"Sir... Alan... please take another officer with you. It's a tough area and two would be safer than one." Sasha glanced briefly over, hoping she hadn't stated the obvious.

Alan nodded his appreciation. "I'm going to ask Officer Rosen to meet me there. He was with me at the Rivera's and speaks Spanish fluently... in case we need it."

Officer John Rosen had been worried about Edgar's grief and anger. He had visited the Rivera's house several times since the murder to offer any help in the way of condolences. He also wanted to be sure Edgar didn't go off the rails. When Detective Sharp called him, Rosen was having lunch at a corner diner in Roxbury. He offered to meet the detective at the housing project in half an hour. The reputation of this project was on his radar, where over half the people were unemployed, most of them on welfare, and the place was well-known for gang activity.

Alan drove into the neighborhood and was not surprised to see several vacant lots, littered with soda cans, plastic bags, and wrappings from junk food. The city had lost funding for many of these communities, leaving people to depend on each other for the basics. There were beat up cars parked along the street and young men in hooded sweatshirts and baggy jeans hanging around a liquor store that was covered with graffiti. Alan was glad he drove his own car and remained unrecognizable, but when Officer Rosen drove up with a police car, he imagined the word spread quickly of police activity.

The building they were looking for was on a busy street and probably convenient for drug sales. It was a system that seemed to work because buyers could purchase their daily or weekly fix and drive quickly away to get on with their day. The project was one of the largest public housing developments in the city, with over 2500 units of low-income apartments. It was old and needed to be redeveloped but was on a long waiting list for city money. The building appeared to be falling apart.

Alan and Rosen walked into the dingy lobby of the building and were greeted by the smell of urine and alcohol. A man was lying on the floor beside the elevator and looked up when they approached him. "It's broken," he said, pointing to the elevator, and laid back down on the floor.

Unwavering, Alan asked the man, "Is there a manager in the building?"

The man pointed to a door across the lobby. As they approached the door a large man with a perplexed look on his face called out to them. "How can I help you officers?" He was walking quickly towards them from the lobby entrance, obviously having spotted the police car. Alan noticed how the man's new tracksuit and white sneakers contrasted with the surroundings. His teeth were capped, but gold fillings were in place, and Alan noticed he wasn't carrying a gun.

"I'm Detective Sharp and this is Officer Rosen. We wanted to ask a few questions about some possible tenants in this building."

"Who? I know everybody here... almost everybody."

"Are you the manager?"

"In a way." He glanced back and forth between the men and then decided to introduce himself. "I'm Pierce Leonard, and I collect the lease money for the building and send it on to the owner. There are others hired to take care of the maintenance."

Alan forced himself not to look around at the filth and wondered how much the maintenance person was paid. "There's been a murder in the area and we're checking out nearby locations for people who might know something about it. Have you heard anything about a young boy being murdered?"

"Yes... I did. I'm sorry it happened, but no one here would have been involved. We're a tight community, and nothing gets past us. So far, I haven't heard a thing."

"Can I show you a CCTV camera video? Maybe you recognize the people involved." Alan took out his phone and handed it to the man.

Leonard looked at the hooded suspects. "No... I don't recognize them... but it's hard to say. If I saw the faces, I may be able to help." He handed the phone back to Alan.

"Is there anyone else we can talk to who might be able to help?"

"No, Detective. I can't think of one person. We're all law-abiding citizens here." The man stared blankly at Alan, as if giving an ultimatum.

Alan looked at Rosen and they agreed to leave. Walking back to the cars, Alan asked, "Did you see his face when I showed him the CCTV? He knew who those kids were."

Rosen nodded. "I agree. What do you want to

do now?"

Alan looked at his watch. He needed to get back to the precinct and meet with Sasha. "I'll let you know. Keep an eye on Edgar Rivera. I'm going to find more out about Leonard and get back with you."

Edgar Rivera was determined to find out who had killed his son. His plan was to talk to members of every gang until he found the murderer. Someone had to know. He had been following three teens in the area for hours. They looked suspicious as they swaggered down the street smoking joints. When they ended up hanging around a deserted park that was known for violence and drugs, Edgar got out of his car and approached them.

"Hey... What you want?" yelled the tallest teen. He stood quickly and displayed a five-inch knife. "Don't come any closer..."

Edgar stopped and raised his hands to show he wasn't carrying a weapon. "I just want to talk. I need some answers."

All three teens laughed. "What you want old man? You a cop?"

Edgar shook his head. "My son was killed, and I want to find out who did it. You heard about the fifteen-year-old who was shot last week?"

One of the teens stepped forward. "We don't know nothing! Get outta here!"

Edgar looked squarely at the teen. "I'll find out who did this. Don't doubt that for a minute!" And then he walked away.

Sasha dropped by the Rivera's house around noon. Mrs.

Rivera answered the door in her robe and nightgown, clutching a t-shirt that probably belonged to Carlos. "Detective... what do you want?" Her eyes appeared red and raw, and Sasha knew this was going to be a difficult conversation.

"May I come in for a moment? I'm only checking to see if there is anything I can do for you."

Mona opened the door and walked slowly into the living room. "I was just doing the laundry and came across this shirt... it was Carlos' favorite." She tried to hold back tears, but a few ran down her face. "I don't know what to do with it..."

Sasha reached out and patted Mona's hand. "Just hold on to it. I'm so sorry for all you are going through. How are the girls?"

Mona looked up and thought. "They're with my mother today. She's treating them to a movie and lunch and letting them stay over. I don't know what I would do without her right now."

"And your husband? How's he doing?" Sasha didn't want to worry Mona about her suspicions that Edgar might be out for revenge.

Mona looked alarmed. "I don't know where he is... he's been gone all night, and I've been calling him over and over."

Sasha nodded. "Okay... let me make a few phone calls and see if I can locate him." Sasha left the room and dialed the police station, just in case Edgar had been picked up. When he wasn't there, she phoned the surrounding hospitals and found he wasn't a patient. She returned to Mona. "The good news is that he's not been hurt... did you call his family and his friends?"

Mona nodded. "They haven't heard from him. Detective, he's very angry and I'm worried he'll do something wrong. I need him here... not out looking for whoever did this."

Sasha was worried, too. Although she didn't want to leave Mona alone, she needed to get this information back to Alan. "Do you have someone who can be with you right now?"

"My neighbor is bringing me lunch today. Everyone has been so helpful."

Relieved, Sasha left the house and stopped to get sandwiches at the deli for herself and Alan. She knew that Detective Mendez always shared meals with him and she wanted to offer the same service.

Alan was entering the precinct when he noticed Sasha with the deli bag. "Do you want to eat first and then we can talk?"

Sasha smiled, "I have a sandwich for you, too, sir, so we can talk and eat."

Alan was surprised with the gesture. "Thank you. Please don't think this is expected of you."

"Sir... Alan... I know you and Detective Mendez had regular lunches together and I'd like to continue that if possible. I believe that sharing a meal stimulates conversation and might lead to deeper understanding." Sasha raised her eyebrows in question. "Don't you think so?"

Alan nodded as they walked into his office.

Alan agreed with Sasha to worry that Edgar Rivera was going to get himself hurt. He understood the grief the man must be feeling, but taking revenge was not going to be the answer. Sasha had looked up Rivera's record and saw he had been arrested for assault several years ago. He spent a few months in jail but otherwise his record was clean. Maybe starting a family changed his perspective. It usually does.

Alan reviewed these thoughts with Sasha. "I'm worried that Mr. Rivera is unpredictable at this time and that his instability could be dangerous."

Sasha agreed. "I'm thinking he may be taking things too far; his car has been gone all night."

"Is this the first time he's stayed out?"

"All night… yes. But he's been going out every night and coming back late. His wife is very worried."

"Okay. Let's find out where he is today. I'll put out an APB for his car."

Alan knew the dangers when someone perceives an injustice and has a strong need to restore balance and punish someone. Usually there's meticulous planning which gives them a sense of empowerment and satisfaction. But it never gave them relief or brought the loved one back. Another problem was that it might create a cycle of revenge in others that could spiral out of control. Alan didn't want to see Rivera, or anyone, go to jail or, even worse, be killed.

As he thought about the mess Edgar could get himself into, Alan got a call from the front desk and was told there was someone waiting to speak with him. Sheila Murphy. Johnson's sister-in-law. Surprised, Alan went to meet her, working through all the possible scenarios for her being at the precinct. As he approached her, he noticed immediately that she appeared to be annoyed, sitting on the edge of a wooden bench, tapping her high heel and scrolling rapidly on her phone. She was a petite woman with highlighted hair and wearing what Alan supposed was a very expensive suit of bone white linen. He stood beside her quietly and with raised eyebrows, asked, "Can I help you? I'm Detective Sharp."

Sheila Murphy looked up and let out a long breath. "I certainly hope so. You called my house earlier and spoke with my young son. I'm Sheila Murphy."

Alan reached out to shake hands, but the gesture was ignored. "Please come to my office and we can talk." Alan kept the door open when they walked through, hoping to discourage an argument. He offered Sheila a chair by his desk. "How may I help you?"

Sheila stared at him with determination. "I want to make this as quick as possible. You said on the phone you were investigating the burglary in our home. I want to know if you have found anything, or anyone involved."

Well, thought Alan, that was certainly to the point. He had only found out about the case! "I called to ask some follow up questions about the burglary. I've read the report and wonder if you've had time to notice if anything had been stolen."

"No. We were away and had every valuable item with us as it happens."

"And have you received any messages, either by phone, computer, text or mail about the break-in?"

"No. I'm not certain about my teenagers, though. I would assume they would let me, or their father, know if someone was harassing or contacting them."

"That's what I need to know. Do any of you believe someone is trying to scare you or might have a reason to get back at you or reveal something to hurt you. It appeared from the report that they were searching for something."

"No. We're a normal family with regular activities. There's no reason for someone to target any of us."

"And I assume you have all spoken about the possibilities and reviewed who might have burglarized your home."

"Of course! We're upset and talked it over. Like I said, I have teenagers and sometimes they aren't as cooperative as you want them to be. But I cannot believe they would be acquainted with anyone who would play such a trick as rummaging through our house."

Alan nodded. "At this point we don't have a lot to go on. We took fingerprints in your house and would like to get you all to come in and be fingerprinted so we might eliminate you. When can you be available?"

Sheila looked horrified. "Look, Detective, I'm not going to have my children fingerprinted. That's out of the question. What else are you doing to get to the bottom of this?"

Alan was getting annoyed with this woman. "We've searched the neighboring CCTV and found nothing." Alan now thought Sheila was wasting his time. He tried another approach. "Why don't you have added security to your home?"

Sheila waved this comment aside. "We did but were dissatisfied with the company and decided to get our own cameras. They didn't arrive in time for our trip. However, we live very close to our neighbors and never imagined someone would rob us when we were away. We even left a key with our neighbor next door to pick up the mail."

"Can I have your neighbor's name and address?"

Sheila took out her phone and scrolled through her contact list. She gave Alan the name of Eunice Jackson. "Detective, I want to get to the bottom of this, but I also want it to just go away. Maybe it was a prank and it's over. My purpose here is to see that you pass me any information you get on the case. Do you understand?"

Alan held her gaze for a moment and then replied, "We will keep you informed. Thank you for coming in." He stood to indicate the meeting was over.

Sheila reached into her bag and brought out a card. "If you need to get a hold of me, please use this number."

Alan took the card without looking at it. He watched her walk out and wondered what the rest of the family was like. And then he thought about Lieutenant Johnson who was also a family member. Must be interesting during the holidays.

Maybe he would hand this case over to the new detective.

SATURDAY OCTOBER 7th

Saturday morning was when Alan called his daughter on the West Coast. The three-hour time difference meant she and her family would be up and planning their day. Lindsay and Sanjay had twin boys who were active in sports and that meant games or practices would take up their busy schedules. "Hi Dad, how are you doing?" Lindsay sounded out of breath.

"Did I catch you running out the door? You sound winded…"

"No, I'm at a soccer game and it's cold and windy. I'm jumping around trying to keep warm. What's up?"

"The usual. How's everyone there?"

"We're fine. Did you think about coming out for Thanksgiving? We would love to have you… and you can bring Maggie, too."

Alan smiled at the thought. "I'll ask her. Right now, she's trying to adjust to a new town and new people. Maybe visiting her friends would be a good idea. Are you sure about this?"

Lindsay laughed. "Dad… we want you to come see us. It's been a while, and the boys miss you."

Alan missed them, too. He had spent the summer months in the Seattle area and had some quality time getting to know his grandsons better. He wanted to keep their relationship close because he knew how quickly time flew and they would be off on their own. "Oh, I have some news. Detective Mendez... Enrique... and his family are moving to Seattle. I'll have another reason to want to visit."

"That's wonderful! Please give me their phone number so I can help them get to know the city. Don't they have three girls?"

Alan was always impressed with his daughter's memory of people. "I'll send you it as soon as I get it from him. They won't leave for a few weeks."

After a few more minutes talking, Alan promised to call again when he could talk with the boys. Now he had to get some coffee and get to the precinct.

Sasha needed to decide if she would go to work today or stay home with her two girls. Being a single mother, she was constantly forced to make challenging choices like this. She had read all the advice from the media about setting boundaries, getting exercise, or engaging in creative pursuits. But her focus was not about personal welfare, it only revolved around her love for her girls and dedication to her job. She was lucky to have her mother close by and always available to take the girls. In fact, tomorrow they did have a full day planned to go shopping and to a movie. She picked up the phone and called her mother.

Alan and Sasha arrived at the precinct at the same time. Both had coffee in hand and what looked like a bakery item from the coffee shop.

Alan looked surprised. "You didn't have to come in today, Sasha."

"I know... but I wanted to get caught up on what

happened yesterday. Has Edgar Rivera returned home?"

"I was just going to call Officer Rosen." Alan placed his coffee and bakery item on his messy desk and made the call. Sasha sat and listened to Alan's half of the conversation, understanding that Rivera was still not home.

"Do you want me to go over and talk with Mrs. Rivera?"

Alan thought for a minute. "She must be worried. Can you call her right now and see if she can give you any idea of where he was going the night he left."

Sasha looked up the number, called, and waited several rings until Mona answered the phone. "Edgar?" she asked in a frantic voice.

"No, Mrs. Rivera, this is Detective Lane. I'm calling to see if your husband has returned. But it looks like he's still missing. Can you give me any idea where he might have gone? Who did he suspect of this crime? And please tell me if he has a weapon?"

Mona let out a sob. "I've tried for hours to think where he might be. He was so upset—we all are—and he kept blaming the gangs. For some reason he got it into his head that Carlos wanted to make money and would try selling drugs."

"Why did he think that?"

Mona's voice was shaking with emotion. "Carlos always wanted the latest shoes and clothes, and we just didn't have extra money to spend. We had heard that kids were being recruited by gangs with the lure of money. Edgar thought Carlos was trying to get into one."

"Do you know what gang it was?"

"We didn't take it seriously. We told him that school

was more important than shoes and clothes." Mona started to cry. "Now Edgar might be out to find the shooter... I don't know what he'll do."

"Does he have a weapon?"

Mona whispered her response. "No, but he could get one."

Sasha looked at Alan to see if she should ask any more questions. He took the phone. "Mrs. Rivera, this is Detective Sharp. We met last week. I'm sorry for everything you're going through, and I want to assure you we are only trying to stop your husband from doing something that will get him in trouble. We've got an alert out on his car. What about family? Does he have a close relative who might be with him?

Mona took a minute to compose herself. "No, his family lives away. He has a friend... his boss... at the shop... Miguel Juarez... who he hangs out with. Do you want his number?"

Alan wrote down the number and promised to call when he heard something. He looked at Sasha. "You did well. I want you to continue to be her friend while I ask direct questions. I'm going to call Juarez now."

Miguel Juarez and Edgar had been friends for years and enjoyed after hour beers a couple times a week. Both men held deep-seated commitment to their families and took pride in their ability to provide for them. They debated often how to balance traditional values with modern expectations because things seemed to change quickly, and it was difficult to navigate these changes.

Miguel was opening the shop garage when his phone rang. He stopped in his tracks when he heard the Detective's name. "Yes, Edgar works here. Is this about Carlos?"

"No, this is about Mr. Rivera. He's not returned home in two nights and we're wondering if you know where he is."

"I haven't heard from him all week. I told him not to come in for a couple weeks... or more... until things are settled. We're all so sad about Carlos."

Alan thanked him and asked him to call if he heard anything.

He turned to Sasha, "If Edgar was looking into gangs, there're several that hang out in the vicinity where Carlos was found. I'll ask for officers to patrol the area and look for him."

Edgar sat at a run-down diner known to be a hangout for gang activity and had the breakfast special. He had slept in his car for two nights and knew he hadn't made a dent in his plan. So far, he had talked with five different gang members in the area and didn't get any results. What was he doing anyway? Did he think he was going to intimidate a gang member? Take someone to the police? He didn't even have a weapon, and he was running out of cash. He had charged his phone in the car and thought about calling Mona to say he was coming home. He finished his food, paid the bill and walked out to his car. He was stunned by a blow to his head, and he fell to the ground.

Sasha sipped her coffee and sat back in the chair. "Where do we go from here, Alan?"

Alan smiled, pleased that they could be on a first name basis. "We need to write things down and look for relationships." Alan went to the white board behind his desk and on one side he wrote down Carlos's name and his family members. He then wrote Miguel's name and phone number, along with both school principals' names. Making a horizontal line in the middle of the board, he wrote Pierce Leonard's name and the address of the project. He also listed the names of the other three teens who were knifed, Jet, Damon and RJ.

"This is as far as we've gotten, Sasha. We're missing a motive. The opportunity may be that Carlos was at the wrong place, and the means was obviously a gun. Call down to forensics and see if they have information on the gun type."

Sasha called and was put on hold. While waiting, she asked Alan who they would talk with next. "I think it's strange that we still don't know the names of Carlos' school friends. Maybe I should speak with Mona again." A moment later the forensic details came in. Sasha reported, "The bullets used look like they came from a 99mm carry pistol. It makes sense because it can easily be concealed in a pocket or a holster and it's small enough for a kid to use."

Alan nodded. "I agree. I've heard that a few gangs rely on that kind of weapon." He wrote this information on the board. "What else do we need to know? What places did Carlos hang out? If he wasn't at school, we need to take his photo around the area and see if he spends time in shops or on the street." Alan picked up his phone and dialed.

"Officer Rosen? Detective Sharp here... I know you're off today, but I was wondering if you had time to take a photo of Carlos Rivera around to some stores and hang outs in the area where he was killed."

Rosen was eager to help. Alan sent him a school photo of Carlos and said he would get back with him in a few hours. "Sasha, I like your idea of speaking with Mona again. Let's get back here around 1:00 and compare notes. I'm going to review the report on the other three teens. They know something, I'm certain of it."

Alan looked through the police reports searching for an address or phone number for the teens. Even though they were frightened by the attacks; they had refused to give names of potential suspects or any information because of reprisals. They knew there was little consolation for anyone caught in the middle of violence when gangs were involved. And in the surrounding project neighborhood, it's not even safe to cross the street sometimes without being accosted and assumed you were a gang member. So far, the three teens had not declared an association with any group.

Wondering if he had the right phone number, Alan found a number on the report and called the oldest teen, Jet.

"Who's this?" demanded a loud male voice who was obviously not Jet.

"This is Detective Alan Sharp, and I would like to speak with Jet. This is the number he gave me."

"Why'd he do that? This is his uncle… is he in trouble again?"

Alan calmly replied, "No, sir, I'm following up on an injury he received last week. I would like to speak with him about the attack."

"What attack? Are you saying he was attacked by someone, and I don't know about it?"

"Sir, I'm not at liberty to consult with you. Do you have Jet's number?"

The man gave a long loud sigh. "Just a minute." Alan waited more than five minutes before the man came back to the phone with the number.

Next, he called Jet. "Yo…what's up?"

"This is Detective Sharp and I'm following up on the attack last week. I have a few questions. Are you free to talk?"

Jet paused, let out a sigh and then said, "I already told you what I wanted to say. Why are you bothering me now?"

Alan knew he had to proceed cautiously if he was going to get more information from him. Many teens feel threatened by law enforcement and refuse to interact, even after they've been attacked. Studies show that juveniles between 15-19 often offend because of their lack of impulse control and their unfortunate exposure to risk factors such as neglect, violence or troubled families.

Alan continued, "Can I meet you somewhere? I have a few more questions about the attack and want to make sure you're doing okay." He hoped this would appease Jet's suspicions. "I could take you to lunch."

The silence on the phone lasted long enough for Alan to believe Jet had hung up. But then he heard, "Okay. Meet me at Spiro's on first. I'll be there in thirty."

Spiro's was a run-down diner in the Roxbury area known for pizzas and lasagna. Alan knew the location but had never been inside. As he entered the place, he was surprised by the low light atmosphere and number of open tables. He glanced at his watch... it was 11:30, so maybe the place would fill up later. He took a table in the rear with his back against the wall to watch for signs of trouble. He worried that the three teens were being followed and wanted to be cautious.

Jet walked in and scanned the room until he saw Alan stand and put his hand up. He quickly walked to the table and sat with his back to the door. "I don't want anyone to know I'm here talking with you."

Alan nodded. "Thank you for coming. Please order some lunch while we talk."

Jet looked at the board on the wall that posted the

lunch menu and ordered a pepperoni pizza and coke. Alan ordered a coke and began questioning. "I need to go over your activities the morning you were attacked. You said in the report that you didn't know Carlos Rivera, the boy who was gunned down, but you were also attacked while running down the same street. What caused the attack? Where were you beforehand?"

Jet took a slow sip from the coke the waiter had just placed in front of him. "I don't know... me and my boys were just hanging around. We were on the street looking for nothing... just deciding what to do."

"Jet, I'm not going to care if you tell me you were trying to buy drugs... that's not what I need to know. But tell me if you believe your assailants were drug dealers?"

Jet looked around and shook his head. "Maybe."

"Okay. Was Carlos with you trying to buy drugs?"

Jet lowered his voice. "You see, Detective, that's not what happens. We don't take some stupid kid and show him what to do. We didn't even know he was following us! Those gang freaks come charging on us and that kid starts running from outta nowhere! We didn't know who he was, and it made us stop taking off and that's why we got knifed."

The pizza arrived and Jet took a big slice. Alan took out his notebook and pen and read from a written page. "Your friends, Damon and RJ, are they okay? I don't have phone numbers for them."

Jet chewed on his pizza and looked suspicious. "Why do you want to know?"

"Jet, we're only following up on the investigation. We need to find the guys who shot Carlos and arrest them. Are you three affiliated with a gang?"

Jet shook his head. "No. At least Damon and I aren't. Not sure about RJ because he kind of lives in different places. We hardly see him."

"Can I have Damon's number?"

Jet shook his head. "No, but I'll tell him you're wanting to talk. He'd get in a lot of trouble talking to cops."

"Why's that?"

"His Dad's in prison and his family's worried about Damon getting in trouble."

Alan nodded. "Okay. Just let him know I asked."

Alan gave Jet his card and stood to pay the bill. "I'll leave now so no one will suspect we were meeting. If you need to talk about anything, just call me. Thank you for meeting me."

Alan texted Sasha that he would meet her back at the precinct. When she arrived, he had already posted Damon's phone on the board. "How did it go with Mona?"

"Poor woman. Edgar hasn't made contact, and she's worried he's hurt. I asked about Carlos' friends, and she gave me a few names, but she didn't know how close they were. It's like what the principal said, he was on his own a lot. I'll give these kids a call. How about you?"

Alan told her about meeting with Jet and finding out that Carlos was following the teens, not hanging out with them. As he was about to tell Sasha to go home and enjoy her weekend, his phone rang.

"Detective, this is John Rosen. Edgar Rivera is in the hospital. He's been mugged."

Sasha immediately called Mona and told her she would pick her up and take her to the hospital. Alan was on his way to Memorial General to speak with Edgar.

Alan and Sasha were waiting to interview Edgar at the hospital. He had been hit hard on his head, and the doctors wanted to keep him overnight in case of a concussion. Mona was pacing in the hallway and asked to speak with her husband alone before the detectives asked any questions. Alan reluctantly agreed.

Five minutes later, a nurse indicated to Alan that they had ten minutes before the pain medicine started to take effect. Alan hurried into the dim room. Edgar's head was bandaged from the blow. "Mr. Rivera," Alan began, "I have a few questions. Did you see the person who hit you?"

"No... he came from behind me." Edgar pressed his head into his pillow as if to stop the pain. "I was walking to my car when I got attacked."

Alan continued. "Where have you been for the last two days, sir?"

Edgar closed his eyes and when he opened them, he looked at Mona. "I'm sorry... you told me to stay home. I'm just so angry about what has happened to our boy. I needed to do something..." he closed his eyes again, and tears started to flow.

Alan continued to probe, "I'm sorry to ask you, but we need to know if someone was following you. This might give us a clue about who did this."

Edgar tried to sit up, but he was in pain. He asked for some paper and a pen. "I'll show you my route." He drew a sort of map that seemed to extend from his house to the area where Carlos was found. "I thought if I searched the neighborhoods, I might know what Carlos was doing. I had his photo, and I asked around." His hand was shaking as he tried to write down some of the stores and park areas he went to. "I asked everyone I saw if they knew him. I don't look like the police, so people stopped and tried to help." He looked over to Mona. "I just couldn't stop. I needed to know what Carlos was doing... why he wasn't in school..." Edgar leaned back on the pillow and closed his eyes.

Alan was impressed. "I understand, Mr. Rivera. I believe I would have done the same. Did you notice anyone who seemed anxious or who followed you?"

Edgar shook his head. "I wasn't looking for anyone like that."

"You were attacked at the diner. Did you notice anyone else there?"

"I was too tired. I was going to call Mona and come home. Did you ask the waitress?" Edgar's voice was beginning to fade.

"Yes, we did. She said there were only two other people there and they hadn't left yet."

Edgar's eyes began to close. The medicine was beginning to make him drowsy and so Alan left the room.

"What now?" Sasha asked.

"I'm just glad to see he's going to be okay. We'll have to get any CCTV coverage from the area and check out the places he traveled. But this can wait. You go home and be with your family. I'm going back to the office to check on my other case."

As the detectives walked to the parking lot, they noticed a man rushing to the entrance. A moment later, Mona was walking out with the man and leaning into his shoulder as he tried to comfort her.

"Who's that?" Alan asked Sasha.

"It's Edgar's boss. I saw a photo of him at the Rivera home. I think he's more of a family friend than a boss."

"Do you think he might be able to help our investigation?"

"I'm not sure. But I'll ask Mona about him when we speak next."

When Alan returned to the precinct, Lieutenant Johnson met him at his office door. He was dressed casually which meant he wasn't there to stay. "Can I have a minute, Detective?"

Alan pointed to the chair by his desk and Johnson sat down.

"How serious do you think this matter is with the Murphys?" Johnson knocked his knuckles on Alan's desk, trying to make a point. "I need some results so I can stop getting calls from my sister-in-law."

Alan put his elbow on his desk and rubbed his forehead. "I've been working on the recent murder case and haven't had time to investigate the burglary. Sheila Murphy was in yesterday and was quite adamant that we find results immediately." Alan looked at Johnson for any signs of affirmation about his sister-in-law's demanding personality. "What do you suggest?"

"Is it possible for you to drop by their home, meet the family, and give them an indication that you're working on it?"

Alan thought for a minute. Should he mention that he was going to assign the case to the new detective? He decided to stall. "I'll drop by their place tomorrow and do an informal report. Maybe I'll learn more and find some leads."

Johnson stood up and shook Alan's hand. "I owe you one."

A MATTER OF TIME

Alan watched the Lieutenant leave and hoped he could get a clue about what was going on. There seemed to be unanswered questions, but Alan wasn't sure what the questions were.

SUNDAY, OCTOBER 8th

Alan had a routine on Sundays. First, he called Maggie. It was only 8:30, but he knew she would answer his call. "Good morning! How are you on this beautiful autumn day?" He winced, thinking he was sounding outside himself.

Maggie smiled into the phone. "It is beautiful. The leaves are getting brighter, and the day is warm. I think I'll go for a walk today. How are you?"

Alan hated to talk about work when they spoke because it seemed to drag the conversation down. "Things are busy as usual... a couple cases are keeping me on my toes." Once again, he winced. On his toes?

"Do you want to talk about it?" Maggie was a good listener and tried to offer advice, especially when she heard tension in his voice.

"Not today. How's your place? The last time we spoke you still had so much to do."

They spoke at length about Maggie's new condo, her daughter and when they would get together again. When they rang off, Alan was in a great mood and so he decided to call his son, Sam.

"Dad... it's early... everything okay?"

Alan looked at his watch and wondered why Sam

wasn't up already. "Yes... I'm fine. I just thought I'd catch up on your week. How are things at work?"

Sam seemed to hesitate, and Alan thought he heard him talking to someone. Of course! Abby was there. Alan hit his head with his hand when he realized he was intruding on their time together. "Hey, you know what, call me later and we can talk."

"No, Dad. Wait... why don't we have lunch today? Abby and I haven't seen you for a while... How about The Parrish in the Back Bay? We'll get there early and save a table."

Now Alan hesitated. "What time are you thinking? I've got one stop I have to make and then I'm free." They decided on 1:00.

Sam was glad his father had called. He had heard some conversations at work that might be of interest in a case he knew Alan was following. He didn't like to share information from the teen center, but he was worried that if he let it go, he might regret it later.

Alan hadn't called the Murphy's before driving to the Beacon Hill address. He didn't want to be put off since he had promised Johnson he would make the call. Hopefully, the whole Murphy family would be available to talk, and they might quickly get to the bottom of what happened and close out this case. When he arrived, Sheila Murphy met him at the door. "Detective, Dale said you were coming by today... please come in." Alan hadn't expected Johnson to inform them of his visit. Or maybe Sheila had called him complaining, once again.

He was escorted through a sun-filled hallway and

turned right to enter an airy living room filled with light from the high ceilings and large front window. A grand piano was elegantly placed before the window, and over a traditional mantel fireplace was an expensive looking black and white abstract artwork. Alan noticed that the formal sofa and chairs seemed to angle towards this piece, revealing its importance. Apparently, Sheila knew how to decorate or had a good designer. She motioned for him to take a seat on a chair and offered him coffee. Alan declined.

"Mrs. Murphy, are the other members of your family available?"

Sheila nodded and called out to her husband and three children. They appeared immediately, obviously knowing they would be summoned to answer questions. Sheila introduced them. "My husband, Tom, and my children, Caleb, Ryan and Melodie."

Alan stood and introduced himself. "I have questions for all of you. I understand that you don't know who burglarized your home, correct?"

Tom spoke quickly. "Obviously we don't, Detective. We're feeling set up and now worried that someone is targeting us for some absurd reason. I have a campaign coming up in my future and wonder if this is a stunt of some sort. Right now, I have my manager looking into anything untoward he can find."

Alan was surprised by this outburst. Why was he so concerned about his campaign? "Was there something you think someone was looking for... maybe to hold against you? Is that what you're saying?"

Tom backed down and shook his head. "No, or at least I hope not. Right now, there's no motive we can think of for someone to ransack our house like that." Alan knew Tom had a solid reputation as a city prosecutor and would be searching for a motive.

"I'm wondering if you did have something they were looking for and didn't find. Have you considered that? Personal papers?"

Sheila and Tom both shook their heads. Tom spoke up first. "When we put things back in order, it seemed random... like someone just wanted to throw everything around and make a mess."

Alan looked at the three teenagers who appeared self-absorbed and uninvolved with the seriousness of the situation. "I'd like to speak with you three alone."

Sheila and Tom glanced quickly at each other for guidance. Tom spoke, "Why's that? They don't know anything, I promise you."

Alan noticed that Melodie, the middle child, rolled her eyes and shook her head. "Even so, Mr. Murphy, sometimes my questions spark a memory that may come in handy."

Sheila and Tom left the room reluctantly and the teens sat next to each other on the sofa. Alan wondered if they were nervous. He began to question them directly. "Do any of you have a reason to suspect someone targeting you? In school? On the internet? Or even an acquaintance?"

All three teens shook their heads. Alan continued. "Okay, let's say this is your parents' problem and you're obviously worried. What are you worried about?"

Ryan, the youngest, raised his hand tentatively. "I think my dad shouldn't be running for office. I'm just nervous about what's happening everywhere in this city with all the racism and gun violence."

Alan was impressed. Emotions always run high in election years, and he knew young people heard a range of opinions. And with the media spreading misinformation and conspiracy theories, parents were expected to control the amount of information and exposure their kids get.

"Do you think your father is in danger?"

Ryan shrugged his shoulders. "I'm just worried. Now that our house got robbed, I don't even want to leave the house!"

Melodie reached over and patted Ryan's arm. "I agree. I'm afraid that someone's watching us. Why would they come into our house and mess everything up?"

Alan could see that the teens were obviously concerned and not dismissing this as a prank. "Have you noticed any person or persons hanging around in the neighborhood area who you don't recognize? A car maybe?"

The teens all shook their heads. Caleb spoke up, "Detective, we live in an exclusive area and know our neighbors. Anyone who even drives down the street to deliver a package is noticed."

Alan nodded slightly. He liked these kids and believed they were worried. "I'll have a patrol car on your street regularly. In the meantime, be aware of your surroundings. Stick together. This may only be a prank, but I'll be taking this investigation seriously."

When Tom and Sheila returned to the living room, Alan asked, "Do you have people who work for you who come around regularly?"

Sheila folded her arms and sighed. "Detective, we have regular employees who help run this house. We have a cleaning person, occasionally a cook, along with a gardener.

Ryan and Melodie take classes after school, but their instructors do not come to the house."

"I'll need the names for all these people. It's just a precautionary idea, especially since politics may be involved." Alan looked at Tom directly. "Do you have any reason to believe you're being targeted by the media?"

Tom shook his head. "Right now, I can't think of anyone who would want to threaten me or my family. I've notified my campaign people and they're going to be cautious."

Alan took down the names he asked for and then told the family he would be in touch. He sat in his car before driving off to write down notes and ask himself, again, how seriously he should take this. Especially if it was a prank or a random act to scare the family. If he was honest with himself, the murder of Carlos was foremost on his mind, and he was, of course, struck by the differences of these two cases. Status was driving the Murphy case, and fear was the basis for the Rivera's. He refused to give short-term results to Rivera's investigation because of any elitist position in the Murphy case. Alan never worked with biases that target financial situations. And despite the worry or uncertainty the Rivera's were experiencing, he believed that Carlos had been targeted for a reason. Were the Murphy's targeted, too?

Alan looked at his watch. He had just enough time to get to the restaurant. Maybe he would surprise his son and be early for once.

Sam and Abby arrived at the popular restaurant as the morning rush seemed to be leaving. The casual atmosphere was consistently friendly, and the food always had fresh ingredients. They took a seat by the window and waited. Five minutes later, Alan walked quickly through the door. "I thought this time I would finally beat you here!" He gave Sam a quick hug and smiled at Abby.

Sam understood that time meant nothing to his dad and just shook his head. "That will be the day, Dad. Maybe when you retire..."

Alan picked up a menu and asked them for a recommendation. Sam and Abby raved about the seafood salad and tacos and waited for Alan to make his choice. When the waitress arrived, they were ready to order. Once their cokes were served, they sat back to relax.

Alan had questions. "Abby... it's good to see you. How's school going?" Abby was in political science, with plans to join the police force. "Only two more quarters and then I'm done. Or... on my way. I'm already locking into police academies."

"Let me know how I can help," Alan offered. "How about you, Sam... anything new at work?" Sam counseled teens at Carla's Teen Center and led an intramural basketball team with kids from around the area.

"My team is number two! They're rockstars! You should come to a game this season. I'll text you the schedule."

"Do that. Maybe when Maggie visits, we can go together."

They visited some more and when the food was served, Sam leaned over and said, "I have some information you might want. Can we talk privately after lunch?"

Alan nodded. They settled into their meals and conversed easily about events and the upcoming holiday. As soon as the food was eaten, Abby excused herself and said she had to get to the library to study. She kissed Sam quickly and said her goodbyes.

"What do you want to tell me?" Alan asked.

Sam thought for just a moment and then leaned in closer. "I know about your case... Carlos Rivera... the kid who was killed. Carla doesn't think it has anything to do with teens we follow, but I heard one of the kids say he knew who did it."

"Did he or she say who?"

"Yeah... Do you know of a kid named RJ?"

"Yes. But that's not who did it. He was one of the kids injured. We can't find him right now. Do you know where he lives?"

"No, sorry. I just heard that name."

"Who was the person who said this?"

"It's a kid named Rico. He's a street kid who seems to know everything."

"Can I talk with him?"

Sam looked doubtful. "You'd have to ask Carla. I've probably stepped over the line right now."

Alan thanked Sam and promised he wouldn't say anything about Sam giving him this information. "Hey... by the way. Are you and Abby going to Lindsay's for Thanksgiving?"

"We might. It depends on her family." They finished their coffee and walked out, each going in opposite directions.

Later that evening, while Alan was relaxing with a glass of red wine, his phone rang. It was Lieutenant Johnson's number. Alan was surprised and answered, "Sharp here..."

"How'd it go with the Murphys today?"

Alan sighed. "I've done everything I can now. I have a patrol car scheduled for more rounds of the neighborhood.

Until we have any evidence, our hands are tied. We just need to wait."

"What do you think of Tom? Could he possibly be hiding something from us?"

Alan was surprised by this suggestion. "Well, you know him better than I do. Why don't you call or go over and find out more. Obviously, they're reluctant to speak about politics or anything connected to it, if that's what you're getting at."

"I guess I will. I was hoping this would be solved by now. Maybe it's just a prank."

Alan wondered again why Johnson was so intent on solving this case. Was there something he wasn't aware of?

MONDAY, OCTOBER 9ᵗʰ

Alan hadn't slept well. The late phone call from Johnson had upset him to the point of a headache. He should have taken a pill to ease the pain, but he kept believing he would fall back to sleep. He laid awake and reviewed how the Lieutenant and he held differing opinions about how to handle a case. Alan wanted to stall until more evidence presented itself, and Johnson always wanted an arrest. So, who was holding the most leverage? Alan felt that after thirty years on the job, he should be given priority to decide how a case moved forward. His style was more traditional and dealt with crime management. He depended on his officers to gather evidence, both visual and physical, from a crime scene and prepare a report so he could carry out an investigation. Alan knew that once he had enough evidence, he would be closer to an arrest. In the Murphy case so far, there was no evidence or even leads.

Johnson relied more on assessing and managing risks by identifying crime patterns. This, too, was dependent on police officers but focused more on surveillance and informants that show the development of the crime patterns. Alan liked this approach, too, but first he needed to interview all involved and search for clues. When he explained to Johnson that he was waiting to interview the people on the list the Murphy's had given him, Johnson disagreed with this approach. By the time Alan arrived at the precinct, he was ready to talk it over with Johnson again.

Alan was surprised when he received an early morning email from Tom Murphy saying he wanted to speak with him today. Maybe there was some more information or, better yet, evidence after all.

Vivian was starting today. Her week of preparing for the new job and trying to pare down her possessions into a manageable pile had given her anxiety overload. Sadie had refused to help, and so Vivian had to box up her room and hope for the best. By the time they moved everything into Anna's basement, they only unpacked their essentials, leaving boxes stacked in the third bedroom. This was meant to be Vivian's office, but that would have to wait.

Vivian arrived at the precinct early. She felt mentally prepared because she was familiar and confident with her knowledge of investigations and case work. Her years of working cold cases had prepared her with current effective tools not available when the original cases were investigated. She also had the opportunity to work with older and retired officers who had years solving cases and had shown her how to review official information such as police records, witness statements, digital forensics data, autopsy and lab reports. These skills were essential now that she was going to be active in current investigations.

A woman dressed in a smart tailored suit approached Vivian at the precinct door. "Are you Detective Collins?"

"Yes. Can you show me where I'm supposed to be?"

"I'm Detective Lane." Sasha held out her hand to Vivian. "Detective Sharp has asked me to show you around and then update you on the cases we're working on."

Vivian was impressed by the detective's straightforwardness and wondered how old she was. Her flawless tawny skin gave no hint of her age, which was a gift all black women shared. As they walked through the squad room, Vivian noticed her composure and confidence and wondered how much experience she had in the department. Without thinking Vivian asked, "How long have you been on the job?"

Surprised, Sasha stopped to think. "Let me see… Do you mean being an officer and then a detective?"

"I guess… yes." Vivian nodded slowly.

"I've been in the police force for over twenty years."

Astonished, Vivian raised her eyebrows and said, "Please tell me you'll be my mentor."

Sasha smiled. "We'll see. In the meantime, let me show you around the precinct and then we can get to work."

Alan saw the two women and walked over to welcome Vivian. He expressed his confidence in Sasha and said he expected Vivian to be in good hands. He returned to his office because Tom Murphy was expected to arrive any minute. He had no clue what the man wanted to talk about.

Tom was nervous about walking into the station. He was known as a thorough prosecutor who wanted every angle to be studied and handled efficiently. Sometimes, that involved putting policemen in difficult positions, especially when serving notice for officers to be summoned to court and maybe put in conflicting situations.

When Alan saw Tom enter the unit, he quickly walked through to meet him. He was aware of all the political noise about potential candidates and their reputations, and Alan didn't want to add to or interfere with public gossip.

"Mr. Murphy, please have a seat."

Alan closed the door to his office. "How can I help you?"

"My gun is missing," Tom confessed.

Alan looked confused. "I thought you were an anti-gun politician."

Tom closed his eyes and shook his head. He then raised his eyebrows as he looked sheepishly at Alan. "Yes, I am. I've had this gun for a while... Sheila and the kids aren't aware it's around. I keep it in a locked case along with other items."

"What other items?"

"Just some old law reviews and papers. Nothing important. The gun is registered... I've had it for several years."

Alan brought out his notebook and asked, "Give me the type and model number. Did they take the case?"

"Yes. But now the word might get out that I own a gun and this might damage my candidacy. I run on a 'no gun' platform."

"What about your political cohorts? You must have a group ready and organized. Could one of them want to hurt your chances?"

Tom nodded and pursed his lips. "I do, Detective, and I trust them completely. We're a small group right now, and I know each of them personally."

"Can I have their names?"

Tom took out a notebook and wrote down five names. "These are the only ones I'm working with now." He thought for a minute. "They're already aware of the burglary, and I don't want them to know about the stolen gun, of course."

"I see the problem, Mr. Murphy, but we don't know for certain that the gun was the motive to burglarize your house. Unless you think that some dirty campaigning is going on."

"I just don't have a clue who would do that." Tom began rubbing his eyes and then shifted in his seat. "I hope that's not the case, Detective. But I wanted to tell you about it. Let's hope it doesn't show up. In fact, if you can keep the burglary out of the media it would also help." Tom stood to leave.

Alan remained seated. "I'll have to report the stolen gun at some point if you want to continue the investigation. Let me know what you decide."

Alan was curious about Tom's political future but didn't want to get into a discussion now. As far as he was concerned, this case needed to be handed over to someone else in the department so he could follow the Rivera investigation. He stood and offered his hand. "We'll do everything we can. Let me know if you find anything else taken."

As Tom walked out of the office, Sasha and Vivian knocked on the door and entered. "Detective, how would you like Detective Collins to start today?"

"I want you to brief her on the murder we're following and consider our options. Mr. Rivera is getting out of the hospital sometime today, and I need you to go to his home and ask more questions." Alan looked at Vivian, "It's good to have you on our team."

Alan watched the women leave and sat heavily down on his chair. He was getting nowhere in both cases. He thought about the lead Sam gave him the day before and considered calling Carla. Just then his phone rang.

"Alan… this is Carla. We have a problem here."

When Alan arrived at the Teen Center, he saw Sidney pull up and park his car. Both men nodded and walked quickly into the Center. Carla greeted them and escorted them to a conference room. Seated inside was a young teen who was gripping the table in front him. He was Latino and wearing the usual large sweatshirt, baggy jeans and expensive sneakers, like most kids his age.

Carla spoke first. "RJ, this is Detective Sharp and Attorney Sidney Miller. They're both here to help you. Please tell them what you told me."

Alan acknowledged the teen with a nod and was relieved to see he was safe. He wondered how Carla knew him but was willing to listen first and ask her questions afterwards.

RJ lowered his gaze and shook his head. "I'm going to be killed if I say anything."

Sidney spoke up, "RJ, I'm here to protect your rights. You don't have to make a statement about a crime if you were involved."

"I wasn't! I was just there!"

Sidney continued, "Okay, then you can tell Detective Sharp what you know."

Taking a deep, pained breath, RJ quietly began his statement, only looking at Sidney. "I was with my guys when that kid got killed. We tried to yell and stop him, but he was too fast and so we started to chase him… that's when we got jumped… and stabbed… and then one of those gang guys pulled out a gun and shot the kid!"

"Did you see who did it?" Alan asked.

"Yeah. And I saw him throw the gun into the bushes,"

"Where's the gun?" Alan knew that the area had been searched, and no weapon had been found.

RJ looked at Carla who walked over to a locked cabinet and opened it. She took out a plastic gallon bag with a gun inside. "I didn't touch it," she said.

Alan and Sidney both shook their heads. Why did this kid pick up the gun? Alan asked him, "Who knows you have the gun?"

"No one!"

Sidney then asked, "RJ, do you have a description of the person who shot the gun?"

RJ nodded. "But I don't know who he is."

Alan asked Sidney and Carla to meet him outside the room. "What do you know about RJ's life? Is he someone you're working with?"

Carla quickly responded, "This is the first time I've met him. Maybe he found out this was a safe place from some of the other teens. All I know is that he walked in here, asked to speak with me and then showed me the gun!"

Sidney reached out to hold her hand. "Are you alright with how this is going? Is there anything you're worried about now?"

Carla looked worried. "I guess I'm okay. I'm going to ask around for any information on RJ and I'll let you know. Right now, I'm just glad to have the gun out of my center and into your hands."

Alan collected RJ and drove him to the precinct to get his statement. When Alan saw Sasha and Vivian at a desk, he called them over and explained the situation. He decided to have them do a formal interview while he tried to get a hold of the one other teen, Damon, to corroborate RJ's story.

Sasha had brought Vivian up to date on the murder and she felt prepared to help. But when she saw the young teen, her heart went out to him. He was small and looked much younger than his sixteen years and seemed boyish with a menacing air. He hid his head under the hood of his sweatshirt and appeared frightened, or annoyed, to be in a police station or to be involved at all.

Sasha introduced herself and Vivian to RJ and asked him if he needed anything to drink. He asked for a coke. Vivian left quickly to get the soda, and when she returned, Sasha was explaining to RJ that she would be recording his responses.

"Tell us first what you were doing on Wednesday, October 4th, the day that Carlos Rivera was killed."

"I already told that other guy everything." RJ slumped in his chair.

Sasha nodded and slightly smiled. "I need it all explained to me step by step."

Once again, RJ repeated what happened that day. His story remained the same and as he spoke Sasha observed him carefully. He was scared, but also vulnerable. He appeared to be a street kid, his clothes were dirty, and his hair and teeth needed attention. Plus, they had been unable to find a current address for him or a school affiliation.

When RJ started to breathe heavily and took a drink from his coke, Sasha quietly asked him, "RJ, when Carlos was shot, what happened next?" Sasha asked.

"This guy stops his car and gets out and runs over to the kid. We see him call on his phone and look around... he sees us and comes over to check to see if we're okay and then goes back to the kid and waits."

"Okay… and then what did you do?"

"I looked back at those guys who had run away, and I saw the gun! The shooter dropped it when he ran off. So, I snuck over and hid the gun."

"Why did you do that?"

"I don't know. For protection… maybe."

"The police didn't find the gun when they searched."

"I hid it in a tree." RJ looked up at the detectives to see if they believed him.

"When did you get it back?"

Reluctantly, RJ knew he didn't have a choice to lie or not. They had the gun now. "After I left the hospital. I needed it."

Sasha nodded as if she understood. "Okay. Let's talk about the gang who attacked you. Did you recognize anyone?"

RJ stared at them. "Only one of them but I don't know his name. I've seen him around. He belongs to a gang."

"Can you give me a description?"

RJ reported what he remembered which was generic and seemed to match most kids that age. "Was there anything about him that was unusual?"

"No."

Vivian thought for a moment and then asked, "Where have you seen him before?"

"Just around… playing basketball… He's tall."

"Where does he play?"

"Anywhere… parks or courts… places where you don't get harassed by police." RJ looked suspiciously at the two women.

"Does this guy have an accent or any marks... like tattoos?"

"Not that I saw. But I never talked with him... just knew he played basketball and thought he was tough."

Vivian continued. "When you say tough, do you mean wanting to hurt someone or just his attitude."

"Both! I was afraid to be close to him."

Sasha questioned something. "If he played basketball, who else knows him? We need to talk with all the players."

RJ let out a long sigh. "I'm going to get hunted if I tell you. Just go out and look for basketball games on the street." He was done talking. He had to protect himself.

Vivian asked, "Where do you live, RJ?"

"Around."

"Do you have a family nearby?"

"No. But I do okay."

"Who sent you to the Teen Center?"

"Word gets around."

"Do you want us to make arrangements for you to stay in a shelter?"

RJ stood to go. "No." He looked around for his backpack and realized he had left it at the Center. "I need to get my stuff... must have left it..."

Vivian quickly offered, "I'll drive you back to the Center."

On the way, Vivian tried to encourage RJ to talk more about his life. He was from upstate New York and was trying to get a job in a kitchen. She told him she would help if he gave her his number. Reluctant to do that, RJ said he would call her if he needed anything.

Sasha reviewed with Alan what they learned from the

interview before Vivian returned. She told him she and Vivian would look for basketball games and see if anyone recognized the description of the shooter.

"I sent the gun to forensics, and we'll have an idea of who it belongs to. Unless, of course, the numbers have been scratched off." Alan looked at his watch. The day had been getting away from him and he still wanted to talk with the Lieutenant about the Murphys.

When Alan walked into Johnson's office, he saw the worry on the Lieutenant's face. "What did Tom have to say?"

Alan sat on the comfortable chair beside Johnson's desk and reported what he knew. "Did you know that he had a gun? He told me it was registered to him, and he kept it in a locked case. Now he tells me it was stolen in the burglary. He seems worried about the publicity. I don't blame him... the media will be all over this if it gets out."

Johnson stared at Alan for a minute, trying to put this new information into his thoughts. "Wait a minute... he's running on an anti-gun platform! How long has he had this gun?"

"He says for years. Do you think Sheila knows about it? Maybe you should go over to speak with them. As far as the investigation goes, we'll have to report the gun missing if we continue."

Johnson rubbed a hand over his face and said, "Okay, I'll make a visit. Maybe they'll just want to step back and forget all about it."

Alan was pleased to think that the Murphy case might end quickly now that Johnson was involved. When he returned to his office, the phone rang. It was forensics. "We have a match on the gun used in the murder. It belongs to

A MATTER OF TIME

Patrick Leonard, AKA Pierce Leonard."

Pierce knew the detectives would be back. It was only a matter of time. His nephew, Alik, was always in trouble and probably on their radar to question. Hopefully he wasn't involved in that murder or even knew who was. Alik was known to be volatile and easily incited to commit crimes, especially when prompted by drugs and alcohol. He had been picked up for robbery at twelve, shoplifting at fifteen and assault at seventeen. His parents had fallen into drugs and hustled on the street to keep their addictions going. They had finally been beaten up, charged with vandalism during a drug deal, and given jail time. It had already been two years, and they had another thirteen months to go. Pierce knew what a mess Alik could fall into. And if he was charged with the murder of that kid, he could see years, if not life, in prison. Pierce needed to talk to him immediately.

Alik lived with his grandmother on the third floor of the building. The elevators were broken again, so Pierce climbed the stairs, stepping over trash and old skateboards that littered the dimly lit hallway. As the manager of the building, Pierce took out his notebook and made a list of the garbage that needed to be hauled away. He tried his best to keep up with leaking pipes, bug infestation, and power outages, and had hired a maintenance person to keep the building clean. That guy hadn't been seen for a week. Pierce made a note to fire him.

When he knocked on Ella's apartment door, the small elderly woman answered. Her bronze wrinkled skin was highlighted with red rouge and her lips were painted a soft pink. She wore a colorful housedress that hung loosely on her thin frame. She smiled when she saw him. "Pierce, please come in and have a cup of coffee with me."

Pierce gave Ella a quick hug and wandered over to sit on a recliner that was covered with a well-used quilt. He knew she made this, along with several others she gave to her friends. He had one at his home. "Aunt Ella, I need to speak with Alik. Is he around?"

Ella shook her head. She was standing in the tiny kitchen and had two steaming cups of coffee in her hands. She walked over and handed one to Pierce and then sat down on a small, tattered sofa. "I just can't keep track of him. And I'm worried... is he in trouble now?"

"I hope not, Auntie. Has he been going to school?" Pierce insisted that all the kids in the building get to school. Because he was the manager, he could make rules like this. It was also up to him to instill the importance of staying off drugs. These two explicit requirements were the only way out of poverty for many of the families who lived in the building and were desperate. Climbing out of poverty demanded discipline, but he knew most families were only able to survive on a day-to-day basis.

Elle shook her head slowly. "I hope he's going to school! He comes home and eats, changes his clothes and then he's out again. I ask him what he's doing, and he promises me he's doing okay. I saw him yesterday around 5:00. He ate some chicken soup and then he left."

"I need to talk to him... it's important. Will you let him know?" He felt sorry for Ella because she was too old to oversee a teenager like Alik.

Ella reassured Pierce that she would. "And you let me know what this is all about!" Her voice rose higher in exasperation. "I'm trying my best to keep him out of trouble."

Pierce nodded but knew it was a hopeless agreement. He admired older folks, like Ella. She had lived in the building for over forty years and found many ways to provide for herself and her family. Sometimes she sold soup and bread to tenants who didn't have time to cook. Sometimes she babysat. Everyone seemed to depend on her.

The building was filled with tenants who relied on small social security and welfare checks they received each month. Some of them had past lives of drug addictions, street hustling, even jail time. They worried about putting food on their tables and trying to keep their kids out of trouble. Many were desperate to find a way to pay the rent because having even a small studio apartment was a refuge.

When Pierce returned to the lobby, he was greeted by two police officers. "Pierce Leonard? We need you to come with us."

Alik Leonard noticed the police car approach the building. He was hidden in an abandoned car parked nearby, afraid that the police had come for him. When he saw his uncle being led out to a police car, he flew into a rage. He hit the wheel of the car with his fists and slammed his head against the back of the seat. He needed to get out of town fast. He reached for a beer on the seat beside him.

Alan met Leonard at the door of the station and took him back to an interview room. He noticed at once how immaculately Pierce was dressed. For being such a big man, well over six-three, his track suit fashion made him appear to be a professional sports figure. He wore two gold chains around his neck and an Apple Watch on his wrist that added a certain amount of wealth to his appearance.

Alan began. "Please, have a seat, Mr. Leonard.

Hopefully, this won't take long."

"Why did I have to be escorted here, Detective? You could have called me to come in and I would have gladly agreed."

Alan nodded. "This is a serious case, and we are in a hurry to wrap things up. I'm sure you understand that we can't wait for people to show up. Do you have a gun, Mr. Leonard?"

Pierce looked at Alan without any expression. "Why?"

"We've found a gun registered in your name at the scene of a crime."

Pierce settled back in the chair. "I do have a registered gun. In fact, I have two. What crime?"

Alan opened a folder and took a photo out. "Does this look like one of your guns, sir?"

Pierce glanced at the photo and blinked a few times. "Maybe. It looks like a gun anyone could have. Why do you think it's my gun?"

"It's registered in your name. When did you last have the gun in your possession?"

Pierce thought for a second. "I need to call my lawyer." He took out his phone and called.

Alan left the room and saw Lieutenant Johnson walking towards him. He explained who he was interviewing and that Leonard was calling his attorney.

Johnson smirked. "I suppose you expected that. A man such as Leonard won't admit to anything without counsel. He's been around long enough to know not to say anything that might incriminate him. What are you going to do now?"

"We're not charging him yet because he doesn't

match the description of the shooter. We only have the gun that matches the case. So now we need to find out who took the gun and committed the murder."

Alan returned to speak with Leonard who was just ending his phone call. "Everything okay?"

"Yes. My attorney will be here shortly."

"Is there anything you would like to tell me before he gets here?"

"Let me explain something to you, Detective, my job is different from yours. I represent the people in my community. Those who have no power, no money, no voice. They hope things will change and someday everything will be equal, when their voices will be heard, when they don't fear the police. If you take away hope, they have nothing." He stopped for a minute before deciding to lay blame. "Teens especially feel hopeless and simply want to blame someone. They become filled with anger and violence. I see it every day..." Pierce shook his head for emphasis.

Alan thought for a moment and then said, "I wish I could do something to help, Mr. Leonard." They were interrupted by loud shouts from lawyer Glen Schuster, who rushed in to talk to his client. He advised Pierce not to say another word and to leave the station immediately.

TUESDAY OCTOBER 10th

Alan arrived at the precinct around 7:30. It was going to be a long day, and he wanted to organize his team and get some questions answered. How would he locate Leonard's gun? Who or what was RJ afraid of? Should he be more concerned about Tom Murphy's stolen gun?

When Sasha walked in fifteen minutes later, he was ready to think out loud. "We need to do some planning. Let's begin with Carlos. He was shot. We have the gun now. We know there was more than one suspect. We have a partial description of one suspect. We need to highlight Carlos... who can we connect him to? He seemed to be a loner, and it may be true that he was following the three other teens for some reason. For what reason? How do we track this down?"

Alan stopped for a minute. "As usual, the evidence is the key. It might shed some light on what happened. If we follow the gun, we'll get some answers. Did Officer Rosen have any luck when he took the photo of Carlos around?"

Sasha read from her notes and shook her head. "It's the usual response in an area known for gangs. No one's talking."

Sasha looked up. "Did Leonard's lawyer shed any light on this? Find out if the gun was stolen or lost?"

"Not a word. I'm going to find out more on the lawyer.

He seems to be a hack... dramatic... insulting. He got Leonard out of here quickly and threatened to sue."

"What do you want me to do today?"

"The other case I've been working on may be wrapped up today. I'll apprise you of the details or tell you if I need someone to work more on it."

Sasha nodded and referred to her notes again. "I have names of friends from Carlos' school who I could interview today. Will that help?"

"Yes. We still need to know why he was in that area."

"Can I help you with anything else or shall we meet back here in the afternoon?"

"I'm going back to the project to talk with people. Take Detective Collins with you and do your best to contact one or two of the friends who knew Carlos. Let's meet back here around 3:oo."

When Sasha left his office, Alan called Sidney and left a message. He wanted to find out more about the lawyer Leonard had called.

Fifteen minutes later his phone rang. "Alan, what can I do for you?" Sidney knew it might be a follow up on the gun and murder.

"Thanks for calling me back. Yesterday I was interviewing a guy about the murder of Carlos Rivera, and he called his lawyer... name of Glen Schuster. Do you know him?"

Sidney let out a slight laugh. "Yeah. He's got a reputation for raising issues rather than solving them, and he tends to complicate all the issues rather than crystallize them. For Schuster... it's all about the money. That's why he takes cases when he knows his client is guilty. He's known to be ruthless about charging them, too. Anyway... he's not one of my favorite people."

"The guy I was interviewing is a manager of a project on the south side. We found out that the gun used to kill Carlos was registered to him. He made no comment about it, just called his lawyer and they walked out. I'm going over there right now to see if I can find more details about the gun. Do you have time to go with me?"

Sidney thought about it. "Do you think you'll need legal advice?"

"I'm not sure. I want to talk with some of the residents and don't want to overstep any boundaries. Do you have time?"

"Sure. But give me an hour. I have some calls to make."

"I'll pick you up at 11:00."

Pierce Leonard used a small apartment on the first floor of the building as an office and sometimes even slept there. His job as manager of the building paid him enough to support his wife and two kids who lived in the Back Bay. He was protective of his family and the last thing he needed was to be in trouble with the law. He knew Alik had joined a gang that was loosely structured but had a strong reputation for violence. Pierce notified his contacts to put the word out on the street to locate Alik. If his gun was in evidence, he suspected Alik knew something about it. How long had the gun been missing? It had been hidden under the office floor along with some cash and legal papers. As far as Leonard knew, no one in the building knew he had this hiding place. It was time to talk with his security team and find out what they knew because things were beginning to get out of control.

An hour later, Leonard heard noises in the lobby.

When he went to check, he saw Detective Sharp standing next to a tall, rather elegant man, who he guessed was a lawyer. "How can I help you... again... Detective?"

Alan introduced Sidney and then said they had come to talk with some residents about the incident of the shooting.

"Why here?"

"Well... it was your gun. If someone here had access to it, we might find our suspect."

Sidney stood by, watching Leonard's every move. He knew guys like this. They had two sides, just like lawyers... the defense and the prosecutor. He could just as easily defend the people he worked for as turn them in. "Mr. Leonard, considering your position in the building, we understand you may be in a compromising position. But to retain authority and instill civic consciousness, it would be in your best interest to let us speak with the residents. How would you like this to happen? Door to door or by calling a meeting?"

Pierce stared at Sidney. "This is a community, not some lowly project. Everyone helps... we share food... we take care of each other. My residents may be poor, but they do not want any violence or want to be involved with something that might put them in danger. Please do not hold them to a lower standard because of that." He looked sharply at both men.

Alan nodded, but at this moment pragmatism was more important than moralism. "A young boy has been shot. That's my priority right now. I need to know who had access to your gun."

Leonard thought for a minute and considered calling his lawyer again. The social issues that entrapped the community—entrenched poverty, domestic violence, guns, gangs—were all about money. But he had to admit that if someone stole his gun to commit a crime, that person needed to be found. "Okay. I'll call a meeting for Wednesday at 6:00." Leonard turned around and left the two men to consider this.

"I'm not sure that got us anywhere," Sidney said as they walked to their cars. "Do you want me to come with you on Wednesday?"

"I'm thinking about asking Carla to come with me. What do you think?"

"Good idea. But I'll bring her."

Alan thanked his friend and drove off to buy lunch before returning to the office. Today, he wanted something simple. He stopped at Subway for a salami sub.

Lieutenant Johnson looked at his watch and decided it was time to make a visit. He called ahead to let Tom Murphy know he was stopping by to talk about the missing gun. He liked Tom but didn't look forward to hearing Sheila's outbursts, especially because he suspected that Tom had never disclosed he owned a gun. If not, she would find out now. They were both outspoken staunch anti-gun activists. When he knocked on the door, Tom answered and invited him in with a handshake. "Thanks, for coming by. Let me tell Sheila you're here." He led his brother-in-law into the kitchen and offered him coffee. Johnson took a mug and then sat at the kitchen table and waited. He was surprised when Sheila walked in. Instead of looking fresh and put together, she was wearing sweats and hadn't applied any makeup. She was wearing black framed glasses instead of contacts and the whole image was of someone suffering from anxiety. Obviously, she knew why he was there.

Johnson stood and attempted to hug Sheila. She waved him away. "We need to stop whatever this is, Dale. I'm going out of my mind thinking this might get out... Why would someone want to hurt us?" And with a muddled mess of emotion, she leaned into Tom and asked wearily, "Why did you ever buy a gun... or not get rid of it ... "

Tom didn't raise his voice, but he was fighting for control. He had never meant for this to happen, and he blamed himself for everything. "I already explained this to you... I've had it for years."

Johnson interrupted. "Listen, the gun might be found. If this is a random burglary, and nothing was here they wanted, taking the gun case was just collateral damage. Something to prove they were successful."

Both Tom and Sheila shook their heads. Tom sat down on a nearby chair and said, "What are we supposed to do? Wait it out?"

"That's all you can do at this point. How are the kids?"

Tom sat back in his chair with a kind of relief. "They're okay. Do you think we should tell them about the gun?"

Johnson had wondered that himself. "I don't think they need to know right now. Unless you suspect they might have a clue who did this... "

Tom shook his head. "We've asked if they suspected someone of robbing us. They seemed just as worried as we are that someone tore our house apart looking for something."

"What about work? You both hold important positions and people know you're running for office, Tom. Could this be a campaign ruse?"

Tom shook his head. "I doubt it... but, you know,

anything's possible if the word leaks that a gun was stolen. Your detective said it would have to be listed as evidence if we moved forward."

"That's right. Think about it and let me know. Right now, the gun is still missing, which is okay, I guess. Hopefully, it stays that way."

Tom stood and shook his head. "Thanks for coming, Dale. We know you have things to do. We'll call you immediately if anything happens." He held out his hand to Johnson.

While driving away, Johnson felt a nagging feeling there was more to the story. Tom hadn't brought up anyone from work, even though a law firm his size could or might be a target for some disgruntled client. If nothing happens this weekend, he'll call Tom into the precinct and go over his list of potential adversaries.

Alan remembered to call Carla and see if she was free to go with him to speak with the residents of the project. "I know this is short notice, but I think your presence would be a big help to the families who are concerned about their teenagers."

"I'm free. Sidney has already called me to say he was going too. Is there anything you want me to say or take note of?"

"I'll leave it up to you. I'm hoping to get some leads on this case."

"Any opportunity I get to talk with families who are going through difficulties helps my kids." Carla had resources available and wanted to inform and explain to struggling communities what rights and opportunities were offered to them.

A MATTER OF TIME

Sasha arrived at Alan's office promptly at 3:00. "I spoke with one of Carlos' friends... Andre Curry." Sasha sat down and pulled out her notebook. "He and Carlos had been friends in Middle School but didn't see much of each other once they were in High School. He said that Carlos always wanted to wear cool clothes and hang out with the older kids." She looked up at Alan. "His parents said this too. But Andre said that there was one mean kid who left school last year and he heard that Carlos was hanging out with him. His name was Alik. Andre didn't know his last name. So, I called the principal to find out about Alik and to get his last name. It's Leonard."

Alan stopped breathing. "Leonard? Alik Leonard? He could be related to Pierce Leonard whose gun was used to kill Carlos! Let's go find him."

On the way to the project, Alan called Officer Rosen to meet them there. He felt the more police backup he had, the stronger they looked. He didn't expect Pierce Leonard to cooperate, but other residents might display defensive attitudes when they found out why they were at the building.

Pierce watched from the lobby as the three officers walked up. They looked determined and he wondered what they wanted. He had tried to locate Alik, but his nephew was off the grid. Hopefully, this wasn't why the officers were there.

Alan once again noted how tall Pierce appeared. He wore his authority well and Alan even respected the responsibility he had taken on, caring for the building. "Mr. Leonard. We're here to speak with Alik. Is he around?"

Pierce pursed his lips and shook his head. "I haven't seen him in a couple of days."

"Does he live in the building?"

"Yes. With his grandmother on the third floor. But I've already spoken with her, and she hasn't seen him either."

"When did you see him last?"

Pierce thought for almost a minute. "I'm trying to think. Why do you want to speak with him?"

"Just a few questions about his relationship with Carlos Rivera."

"The kid who was shot... Alik didn't krow him!"

"We believe they knew each other. When do you expect to hear from him?"

"I'm not sure. Sometimes he takes off for a few days. He's not in school, so I've told him he has to get a job."

Alan was impressed that Leonard seemed to want to help. But family always came first, and Leonard might want to appear to help but would also want to protect Alik. "Do you have a photo of him?"

"No."

"Can I speak with his grandmother?"

"She's out shopping right now. The women go together on Tuesday mornings."

"I'll need Alik's phone number."

Pierce took out his cell and read off the number. "He never answers his phone."

Alan nodded. He quickly sent a text to the number. *"Call me."* Hopefully this would arouse his curiosity. Alan looked at the two other officers and indicated it was time to leave. "We'll be in touch, Mr. Leonard. And oh... let's postpone that meeting set for tomorrow night."

Alan spoke with Officer Rosen before he got into his car. "I want you to follow Leonard. My guess is he'll contact

Alik and go meet him later. Are you free to do this?"
"I've arranged with my superior to help with your investigation. I'll use my own car, so I won't be noticed."

Alik looked at his phone text and didn't recognize the number. Call me? Who was that? His gang had a signal they used, and that wasn't it. A second later he got another text... *Stay away. I'll find you.* Alik knew this was from his uncle. Something had gone down. He had to stay hidden.

WEDNESDAY OCTOBER 11ᵗʰ

Sasha met Alan first thing. She looked at the timeline board as she sipped her coffee, hoping it might finally shed some light on the case. Alan had an idea. "I think it's time we spoke with Mona and Edgar again. Let's question them about Alik Leonard."

"Do you want me to call?"

"No, let's just go over to their house. If we come unannounced, maybe they'll be more candid with us."

Mona was still in bed like most mornings since Carlos had been killed. Nothing was getting any easier and she felt exhausted, especially now that Edgar had been attacked. Edgar was worried and hoped she would at least get dressed, if only for the girl's sakes. He had offered to call her doctor that morning to get her some medication.

The knock on the door startled him. When he opened it and saw the detectives, he folded his arms in front of him as if to block their entrance. "What do you want now?"

Alan understood the man's grief. Being angry with the police was part of going through the cycles. Why hadn't they protected their son? Why had they let this happen? Who did this awful thing? Alan had heard it all.

"We're sorry to bother you, Mr. Rivera. We're checking in and asking a few more questions. May we come in?"

Edgar stared for a moment and then moved away from the door. "Mona is still in her room."

Sasha spoke up. "I'll go and see her. Can I bring her a cup of tea?"

Edgar looked almost grateful. "She likes a little sugar."

Alan followed Sasha into the kitchen, hoping this would be a comfortable place to speak with Edgar. They sat at the small kitchen table. "We've spoken to a friend of Carlos... Andre Curry... do you know him?"

Edgar shook his head. "They were friends in middle school. I haven't heard Carlos mention him in a long while. What did he say?"

"He said that Carlos was hanging around a kid named Alik Leonard. Do you know him?"

Edgar shook his head. "Where's he from? Around here?"

Alan didn't want to give any additional information to Edgar, knowing that he might go after Alik. "No, he's not, but we're trying to locate him. Did Carlos spend time away from the house after school? On weekends?"

"Yeah... we didn't know what he did a lot of the time, but he always came home when we asked him to. We were giving him some space... you know. We encouraged him to play a sport or even find a job. We worried he was a loner."

Alan recognized Edgar's despair and wondered how he would handle it if anything happened to Sam. "How are the girls holding up? It must be very difficult for them."

"They're very upset. We let them stay with their grandparents for a while longer. My parents live in the Back Bay. I'm trying to get Mona to go over there and see them."

Edgar looked so sad, that Alan had to glance away.

"We'll keep you up to date. In the meantime, if you hear anything at all that might help, please don't hesitate to call me or Detective Lane." Alan heard Sasha walking down the hall and knew she was finished speaking with Mona. They walked to the door and shook hands with Edgar.

"Did you find anything out from Mona?" Alan asked.

"She said Carlos did talk with her about someone named Alik. He spoke as if he was a hero or someone who had all the answers. She asked him to invite Alik over, but Carlos didn't want to. She was just glad to know he had a friend."

Alan let out a sigh. "From what you found out from Andre, Alik bullied Carlos. Poor kid... he probably didn't realize the bullying if he got the attention he wanted. Now we need to find Alik."

Alik decided to take a chance and meet with his uncle to learn why the police wanted to talk with him. He texted Pierce and suggested they meet at a diner in Hyde Park. It was off the grid where he wouldn't be seen, especially if the police were after him. Maybe his uncle would help him get out of the city for a while.

When Pierce entered the diner, he saw Alik sitting in the corner, reviewing the menu, or hiding. He walked over and sat down. Alik jumped and then relaxed when he saw it was his uncle. "What's happened?" he asked.

Pierce stared at him and then shook his head. "What have you done? Did you take my gun?"

Alik started to lie but then decided to say nothing. He just sat back in his chair and motioned for the waitress. After he ordered a hamburger and coke, he looked at Pierce and boldly stated, "What? Are you accusing me?"

Pierce waved the approaching server away. He was raging inside but he knew if he lashed out that Alik would feel threatened and become aggressive. "Alik, I need to know if you took my gun. The police have it." He looked for his nephew's reaction to that.

Alik shrugged. "Why would I have it? Did you lose it or something?"

Pierce hated the smug attitude Alik posed. "Listen, if you're involved in the murder of that kid, you're in big trouble. I can get you a lawyer right now if you know anything about how that kid was killed. The police think you knew him. Did you?"

Alik shook his head. "Nope."

Pierce knew he was lying because he had a self-satisfied smirk on his face. This kind of arrogance attempted to display dominance but generally hid great insecurity. Alik had always been insecure. He failed at school after being tested for dyslexia and behavior disorder. That led to truancy. Alik knew his uncle demanded an education, so he had kept a distance from him. Pierce hoped Alik wasn't the one the police needed to find.

Pierce continued to stare at Alik. "Okay, we'll go talk with the police and get them off my shoulders. If you're telling me the truth, then you'll be fine."

Alik watched the server bring his food. He carefully took the hamburger bun apart and added catsup while shaking his head. "No way. I'm not going to the police for anything." After taking a big gulp of coke, he looked at his uncle and said, "You can't make me go... I have rights. And you won't turn me in... I know you won't."

Once again, Pierce's anger flared inside. He was just

about to lay into Alik when someone came up from behind him. It was Officer Rosen. Pierce had been predictable and led Rosen right to his nephew. "Alik Leonard... I need to take you in for questioning."

It was close to 5:30 when Rosen and Alik entered the precinct. Alan and Sasha were waiting and pointed to an interview room, advising Rosen to leave Alik there. Alan thanked Rosen and let him go to write up the report.

Alik started fuming. He began pounding his fists on the metal table. Had his uncle betrayed him? If his uncle was on his side, he should call a lawyer and get him out of this mess. Alik was determined to say nothing to the police, even if he had to stay at the precinct all night.

Alan was aware of Alik's temper and let him fume. All they had on him was that he knew Carlos Rivera and he matched the description of the shooter. That wasn't enough to keep him. He looked at Sasha and said, "Let's get this over with. I want this kid to know we're watching him and hope he makes the wrong move."

They entered the room and sat across from Alik. Alan pointed to the recorder, "Alik Leonard, I'm going to tape this interview." He pushed a button and began, "We only have a few questions. How did you know Carlos Rivera?"

Alik said nothing. He sat with his arms folded tightly and looked down at the table.

"Do you own a gun, Alik?"

Alik tensed but didn't respond.

"We've spoken to some teens who were hurt in an incident last week and they might recognize you. What were you doing on Wednesday, October 4th?"

Alik remained motionless.

Alan looked at Sasha. She nodded and asked the next question. "Because you're eighteen, Alik, we can keep you overnight. Do you want to call a lawyer?"

Alik looked at her and smiled. "My uncle already has a lawyer. He'll get me out of here."

Just then they heard the loud voice of Glen Schuster demanding to see his client. Alan went to the door and let the lawyer enter. "Come on Alik... you're free to go. They don't have a reason to keep you."

Alik grinned and slapped his fist on the table. "It took you long enough to get here!"

Annoyed, Schuster grabbed Alik's arm and led him forcibly out the door.

Alik had to find a place to stay. He knew his grandmother would be upset if he returned home so late and would ask too many questions. He thought about bunking with one of the gang but kept warning himself not to trust anyone. So, he decided to sleep in that old, abandoned car one more night. He had stuffed some blankets and clothes in the trunk last time he was there and hoped no one had stolen them.

He spotted the car on the road by the park, hidden behind some overgrown bushes, weeks ago. He wondered why it hadn't been towed away, but considered it was his luck to still be there.

He hadn't told anyone about the car because if his gang got hold of it, there would be nothing left. They would tear it apart. He was getting tired of the stupid petty crimes they played at. He always knew it would lead to something bad... and it did. That kid was shot and died. Alik never meant for it to happen... he'd been pushed, and the gun went off. It wasn't his fault!

The car was cold and damp. Even the blankets felt wet. Alik guessed the car was leaking somewhere, maybe a cracked window, although he didn't see a crack when he got in. But it was dark.

As he drifted off, he thought about how disappointed his grandmother would be if she knew he wasn't coming home tonight. She worried about him constantly because she knew he hung out with the wrong crowd.

This would be the last night he spent in the car. He had some cash, not much, but enough to take the train out of town. He knew a guy who lived in upstate New York who might give him a couch for a while.

He'd miss his grandmother. She was the only person alive who believed he could turn his life around. She thought he was smart. This made him smile as he huddled down into the seat and tried to generate some warmth. He was street smart, not school smart.

THURSDAY, OCTOBER 12th

The phone woke Alan at 5:30am. He coughed a couple times to clear his throat and then answered, hoping it wasn't bad news. It was Lieutenant Johnson. "Alik Leonard has been found dead. He was beaten to death."

By the time Alan arrived at the precinct, more details were available. Alik had been found near the project, apparently hiding out in a car. His body was noticed by an early morning jogger who saw a lifeless body in the backseat of an old, abandoned Cadillac. Forensics had been called, and the body and car had been turned over to evidence. No object was located that might have killed him. The ME guessed the beating occurred in the early morning.

Alan found Sasha and they decided to go speak with Pierce and Alik's grandmother.

Pierce had heard the sirens earlier and hadn't been concerned, since it was a regular occurrence in the neighborhood. He was going through his list of chores when he saw the detectives arrive. "What now?" he said with an exasperated tone.

Alan suspected he didn't know about Alik. "Can we talk privately?"

Pierce picked up on the seriousness of the tone and led them into his office. He didn't offer them a chair, just stood and waited to hear what they had to say.

Alan looked uneasily at Pierce. "We found Alik beaten to death this morning. I'm very sorry."

Pierce didn't breathe. His eyes darted back and forth between the detectives and then he dropped into a nearby chair. "How? Where? Who..."

Alan shook his head. "We have no answers yet. He was found in an abandoned car a couple blocks from here. It appeared he'd been sleeping in the car because we found some clothes and blankets. Can we speak with his grandmother?"

Pierce looked up and his eyes wandered around the room. "This will kill her. She's tried to keep him safe, but he kept rejecting all her help." Pierce rubbed his face with both hands and shook his head. "I'll take you to her apartment.

Ella was up early and watching the news. She'd heard the sirens in the morning but didn't think much about it. Although she worried about Alik, she knew he would come home when he was hungry and needed some clean clothes. He always did. When she heard the knock on her door, she thought it was probably Alik because he had lost his key, again.

Pierce stood at the door and looked sadly at Ella. "We need to talk, Ella, I'm sorry to bring you some bad news."

Ella stood rigid and stared at him. "Please don't tell me it's about Alik." Tears began to fill her eyes, and she felt unsteady on her feet. Pierce led her back into the room and sat her on the small sofa. Sasha stepped into the tiny kitchen and started some hot water for tea.

Pierce held Ella's hand and told her all he knew. "They found him sleeping in a car. He was beaten badly. We're going to find out who did this and make them pay."

Ella continued to cry. "Why didn't he listen to me? I kept telling him to get a job and make some money... but he just didn't listen." Alan offered her a handkerchief; one he carried in his pocket for times like this. It was always difficult to watch someone break down, and this was the least he could do. Ella held the handkerchief to her eyes and sobbed.

Sasha put a cup of tea on the small table in front of Ella and then sat beside her. "We are so sorry, Mrs. Leonard. Do you have any idea why Alik was in the car?"

Alan was pleased that Sasha had taken the lead. He decided to sit back and see how far they could go before the awful tragedy took over and Ella wasn't able to speak.

"He sometimes didn't come home. I never knew what he was doing or where he was..." Ella tried to dry the tears that were streaming down her face. "Pierce... what do you think he did to deserve this?" Her voice had risen, and she was staring at her nephew as if he was to blame.

"Aunt Ella, I don't know. But I swear to you I will find out and when I do, they will be sorry."

Sasha continued quietly to probe. "Do you remember the last time you spoke with Alik, Ella?"

Ella looked down at her teacup, which sat untouched. "I don't know... have you talked to him, Pierce?"

Pierce didn't want to let her know about his conversation with Alik at the diner or about the police questioning him. He shook his head and said it was probably sometime over the weekend when he had seen Alik.

Ella sobbed. Sasha put her arm around her and looked at Alan. He shook his head, slightly, to indicate they were through.

Alan turned to Pierce. "Is there someone you can call who will stay with her?"

Pierce took out his phone and called Ella's best friend who lived on the second floor. "She'll be here in a minute."

Alan nodded. "I'd like to ask you a few more questions. Can we go to your office?"

Sasha offered to stay with Ella until the neighbor arrived. Pierce was reluctant to leave but promised Ella he would return soon. He knew as soon as the word got out, residents would be flocking to Ella with food and comfort.

As they walked down the stairs, because the elevator was not working, Alan began to question Pierce. "Again, I'm so sorry. The last time you saw Alik, did you ask him about the gun?"

Pierce blinked several times as if trying to remember because he knew he and Alik had talked about it. "No... I just reminded him to stay out of trouble. He said he was looking for a job." That was also a lie, but he wanted the detective to go a different direction."

"Do you know where he was looking?"

"Where all the kids look... grocery stores... gyms... car wash... anywhere that will give them a chance."

When they arrived at the small office, Alan continued to probe. "Okay... let's say that he was job hunting... Why do you think he was sleeping in that car? Was he afraid to stay with his grandmother?"

"He did that sometimes... when he was out late. He knew there were abandoned cars around here, and he just used them. Lots of kids do that."

"We found some drugs on Alik... not much... Do you know where he bought drugs?"

Pierce stared at Alan. "How would I know? My rule is to stay off drugs."

"I appreciate any help you can give us to find who did this. You have an ear to the building and might hear something we need to know."

Pierce nodded and waved slightly at the people who were congregating at his door. "It looks like the word is out. I need to talk with my people and help them deal with this."

Alan understood and walked out of the office to wait for Sasha to join him in the lobby. When she arrived, they both looked discouraged. "I have no leads," Alan said. "If Carlos thought of Alik as some kind of hero, I bet there are other kids who thought so, too. It's time to find those kids."

Vivian was waiting for Sasha to get back to the precinct. When she heard about the murder of another teen, she hoped to be involved with the investigation. Alan saw her waiting and called her over.

"I have some research I need you to do."

"Yes, sir, I'm ready to work."

Alan rifled through the notes he had taken and found the registration number of Tom Murphy's gun. He asked Vivian to run down anything she found on it. "The gun is missing and needs to be found. It was stolen in an attempted burglary along with some personal papers. I want you to investigate the owner's background, too." As he handed her the information, she heard the urgency in his voice. "This is confidential, as I expect you know."

Alan waited longer than he wanted for the medical examiner's preliminary report to be done. Two teenagers were dead. He was getting frustrated with the lack of information and evidence in both cases. He called Sasha from her desk and tried to hide his growing anger.

Sasha heard the tone of his voice and slowly entered the office. "What's wrong?" she asked in a motherly tone, hoping to calm her boss's nerves.

"We just don't have enough to go on with these cases." Alan slammed his hand down on his desk for emphasis, toppling files onto the floor. "We have a gun but now the suspect is dead. Does the grandmother know anything else? Why was he sleeping in his car? Who gave him the drugs? Who followed him? And... maybe most importantly, who called this in?"

Sasha paused to give Alan time to settle before reviewing what she knew. "It looks like the caller's probably in the wind right now. You know how it goes... people don't want to get involved. Most callers believe they'll be accused of the crime if they do. And as far as we know, Alik slept in his car when he was drugged and didn't want his uncle or grandmother to know."

"So, who were his dealers?" Alan demanded.

"We're trying to find this out. There are several dealers in the area and so I think we should send one of our officers out to see what they can find. It should only take a day, maybe two."

"Good idea. Do this and get back to me." Alan dismissed her with a slight wave of his hand. And then he called her back.

"I'm sorry to be so angry. I think I'm getting to the point where these cases are getting too personal. Thank you for understanding and following up."

Sasha nodded and left. She had never seen Alan so discouraged about a case. Hopefully, he wasn't thinking about retiring.

Alan realized that being angry and feeling he was losing control of the investigation made him feel vulnerable and disheartened. He glanced hurriedly at the clock and decided to call Maggie.

"Alan! It's wonderful to hear from you, especially when I know you're at work. Is everything okay?"

Alan smiled to hear her support. "I just had a conversation with Detective Lane that left me feeling out of sorts about it."

"What was the conversation about?"

"It's about losing control of the cases we have, and I guess I just wanted to blame someone or something. Every time we get one step ahead, we lose three more."

Maggie took a minute before she responded. "I think we've talked about this before... how to avoid judgement, especially about yourself."

"I know we have... and I seem to still set up walls when questioned about how my cases are moving along. Sasha wasn't questioning me... I'm just grappling with the unpredictability of the cases." Alan expected to make decisions without experiencing so much doubt or having to admit mistakes or apologize when wrong. He let out a long sigh. "I need to learn how to not take things personally."

"As usual, Alan, you're harder on yourself than anyone ever would be. Your job demands some vulnerability, especially with someone you trust. You and Enrique had that kind of relationship, and I know you miss that."

"I do miss him. We both had the same view of ourselves *'Here I am—this is me.'* Our approach was to lay everything out clearly and concisely... It worked for us."

"Maybe it's time to apologize to Detective Lane and let her see more of your vulnerable side. Tell her you want to share more of the nitty gritty of the cases frankly and hope she will too."

"You're right. Let me ask you another thing. Do you think this is all about getting closer to retirement? Maybe my days here are numbered... I'm feeling burned out."

Maggie had heard this several times lately. "Have you decided on some second act? I can't imagine you sitting at home all day." Maggie paused. "Look... I know you're busy now and so let's talk about this later."

Alan nodded into the phone. "Thanks for letting me spout off to you. I haven't even asked how your day's going."

"I'm right in the middle of recipes for the catering party I've been asked to do. Please remember you're going to taste test for me this weekend."

"I'll be there!"

Vivian was pleased to have a case to investigate, even though it seemed to be low key to her. Sasha hadn't mentioned needing to find a missing gun, so Vivian wondered if it was personal to Detective Sharp. When she looked up the Murphy's address on the gun registration, she was surprised it was a Beacon Hill residence. She didn't recognize the name of the gun owner and had no idea of his status as an anti-gun activist but assumed the family was wealthy. Why the Murphys? She then read that Tom Murphy was a leading prosecutor in the city and was running for office in a couple months. If that was his gun, why all the secrecy? And then she saw it, his platform included anti-gun initiatives. She started to put the pieces together.

Tom Murphy had no significant details, so Vivian

decided to look up Sheila's profile in case anything jumped out. Vivian read that she grew up in New Haven, Connecticut and attended Yale University. She was from a wealthy family, had a few driving tickets, but nothing out of the ordinary. But something triggered the detective's memory. Sheila attended Yale University around the time a young co-ed had been killed. Vivian had a sharp memory for facts and could grasp information and retain and recall it when required. Therefore, access and flexibility of remembering events and people came easily to her. She seemed to remember the slain co-ed's roommate was named Sheila.

Vivian called over to cold cases in Hartford to speak with one of her pals from the unit. "Hey, Ken, do we still have a report back in the late nineties from an incident in New Haven or Yale? A young co-ed was killed."

Ken said he would get back to her when he had a minute.

Thirty minutes later an email arrived on Vivian's computer. She read about the investigation involving a co-ed at Yale, a junior who had gone missing during finals week and had never been found. During those years there were no security cameras or cell phones to follow up on. Her roommate had been out partying with her but suffered a potential memory loss about when she had last seen her. Talking with people at the party, the police found there were no consistent answers about who she was seen with or when she left the party. The case lingered on in the news until the holidays, when only seasonal stories were highlighted. Yale University used all their resources to hide the school's name from the press. They had gained attention for other problems plaguing the school.

A MATTER OF TIME

Yale University ranked third in North America and had graduated notable alumni including presidents and Nobel Prize winners. Known for its academic excellence, the school's also known for its competitive atmosphere, and over the years, the college has faced significant criticism for their mental health policies. It's said that the wait list for therapy on campus could be months, and individual sessions might run only 30 minutes. Students were sometimes forced to hide their depression to stay in school. As a result, the school had not cooperated with the investigation of this young co-ed.

Vivian looked through the photos that were taken of the missing co-ed and the students who were interviewed. And there she was. Sheila Sanders. The roommate.

Vivian wondered if she was going off course by looking through Sheila Murphy's files. It wasn't her gun that was stolen. In fact, did she even know about the gun? Sometimes spouses hid weapons because of disagreements concerning accessibility, or in this instance, other people finding out. Why did Vivian need to learn more about Sheila's family? Looking through the cold case file she came across a detective she recognized. Laura Fain had been a lead on this case and would probably know more details. Vivian looked up her number and called.

"Well... Vivian... it's been too long! How are you?" Laura had a good memory, too.

"Did you hear I'm in Boston now? Joined the detective team under Sharp."

"You're in good hands with him. How can I help you?"

"I'm looking back on a cold case in New Haven, Yale in fact, and I see that you led the investigation. A co-ed was missing and never found. I see her roommate was Sheila

Sanders... Do you remember anything about this case?"

"I do remember and wish we had solved it. I always wondered about the roommate. I gathered some facts about her in case I suspected her of being involved. Let me pull up what I had." A minute later she read from her computer, "Sheila's father and grandfather were Yale graduates who made their money in investments. Because she was the oldest in the family of two girls, she was encouraged to follow in their footsteps and carry on the family name. The workload, complex material and higher expectations along with frequent exams, left her feeling overwhelmed. She excelled only because of the hours she spent in the library or with tutors. What little time was left for socializing was spent sleeping. Sheila graduated a semester behind her peers, but she was the lucky one. A job was waiting for her in the family firm." Laura scrolled down on the report. "That's about it. Why is this on your radar?"

"Actually, it's not important. But thanks anyway for the information." When they hung up, Vivian made a few notes and then continued to search for the gun.

FRIDAY, OCTOBER 13th

Alan was always amused how seriously people took Friday the thirteenth superstitions. Even his daughter, Lindsay, dreaded this day, but Alan thought it was due more to her classroom students getting into mischief than about anything else. On the other hand, there was the criminal element of the day, and he worried some people might use this date as an opportunity to commit a crime. It had happened before.

Vivian met him at the office and followed him in. Before he had a chance to put his coffee down, she began talking. "Sir, I think I might have found some information about the stolen gun that you should know about."

Alan wondered if her enthusiasm was overblown since this was her first case. "Okay... let's hear it." He sat down, hoping this might be important and the case would go away.

"The gun was purchased legally ten years ago by Tom Murphy. I looked through the National Crime Information Center database and found he was the only owner. I was able to discover and confirm the manufacturer, the approximate year it was made and model. I'd like permission to search pawn shops and gun shows in the area. I'm already checking crime reports to hope the gun hasn't ended up in the wrong hands or might be trafficked. Should I make a visit to the

Murphy home to question them?"

"Before you go any further, let me run this by someone. I'll get back to you about how to proceed with this information. Good work, Detective Collins."

Although Vivian was disappointed, she stood and saluted Alan before she left his office. Alan grimaced. *Why does she keep doing that?*

Sasha entered Alan's office with a question. "What was that about?"

Alan didn't respond except to say it was another case. He wanted to keep their full attention on the murders. "We need to locate people, teenagers and gang members probably, who knew Alik. If we think he was a leader of sorts, maybe we'll find someone who had a grudge and wanted him killed. But first, we better go and talk with Edgar Rivera and find out what he was doing early Thursday morning."

An hour later the detectives were on their way to the Rivera's. Hopefully, Edgar would be home, and they could eliminate him from the suspect list. Although he had a motive, they both believed he understood the consequences of revenge.

Mona answered the door wearing a beige, well-worn sweatsuit. She looked a bit more rested than the last time they saw her. "Do you know who killed my boy, detectives?"

Alan shook his head. "May we come in for just a minute? Is your husband home?"

Mona opened the door wider and yelled for Edgar. He appeared from a bedroom and looked surprised to see the detectives. "What now?" he asked harshly.

Alan understood how cautious and suspicious Edgar felt. "We just have a few questions and a report to give you."

Mona led the way into the kitchen. They sat at the small table and Alan began. "Alik Leonard was found beaten to death early Thursday morning. Do you know anything about this?"

Edgar and Mona looked at each other astonished. "That's the kid who shot Carlos?" Mona asked.

"We believe so." Alan looked at Edgar. "Have you ever met Alik?"

Edgar shook his head. "You don't think I had anything to do with this do you?" He appeared to be struggling to hold his temper in line.

"We need to ask where you were on Thursday in the early morning. And late Wednesday evening."

Edgar stood and began pacing. Mona looked alarmed. "He was home with me."

Edgar stopped in front of Alan. "Does this mean the case is dropped? That we don't get to see someone punished for what they did?"

Alan knew this question would come up. "Alik was never charged for shooting Carlos, Mr. Rivera. He was a suspect, and the investigation was still in the early stages. I'm sorry. If I can confirm that you were home all evening on Wednesday and Thursday morning, we can leave and let you get on with your day."

Mona looked apprehensively at her husband. She knew he wouldn't let this go. Someone had to pay for what they did. She repeated her statement again. "Edgar was home with me."

Alan and Sasha stood to leave. Sasha put her hand on Mona's shoulder. "Please call me if you need anything."

When they left Sasha asked Alan, "Do you

believe him?"

"I want to," Alan replied. "I hope he was home."

"Who do we talk to next?"

"I want to chat with Jet and RJ again. If they were following Alik that day, they might know more about his daily moves. Did we ever find out where Damon lives?"

"I've tried to locate him, but without success. Didn't you say that Jet had a cell number for him?"

"Yes, that's right. I'll try and get it from him this time. In fact, why don't you interview Jet? Maybe he'll give you the number. I've got something to check on so let's meet back after lunch."

Back at the precinct, Alan immediately went to the Lieutenant's office. Finding him there, Alan asked for a few minutes of this time. "Right now, I'm involved with the Rivera case, and so I've assigned the Murphy case over to my new detective. She's been tactfully searching for the gun since the Murphys don't want to go public over it. She seems eager to handle it, if that's okay with you. I've not mentioned your involvement."

John gave it a moment's thought. "Okay, go ahead and have her report back to me. Anything I can do to help with your murder investigation?"

Alan considered it, appreciating the offer. "Thanks for asking. Detective Lane and I are following leads. We're getting no cooperation from the family of Alik Leonard, unfortunately. I just hope they don't try to seek revenge their own way."

"Okay. Keep me informed."

Alan returned to his office and studied the white board details, looking for anything that would help solve these murders. Two teens were killed days apart. If Alik did kill Carlos, then revenge was certainly a possible motive. But who would know how to find him and why beat him up? Alan needed to know more about Alik and his gang affiliations. And he needed to talk with Damon.

Alan wondered again what motivated Alik to kill Carlos. The other two suspects had never been located, and if they belonged to a gang, they'd never be found. Why shoot an innocent kid like Carlos?

So far, everyone Alan spoke with said Carlos was a good kid, but he seemed to be searching for an identity and had a hint of rebellion. The tech department hadn't found any clues on his social media that helped the case. That seemed odd because most teens were glued to their phones and iPads. Alan knew that social media and its use by teenagers was complicated and depended on many factors. While there were certain benefits, there was also a broad range of pressures and negative consequences to consider. It was up to parents to establish a dialogue to ensure their teens wouldn't get rebellious. What restrictions did the Rivera's have for Carlos? Alan called down to tech.

"Did you find anything on Carlos Rivera's phone to indicate he had another cell?"

"No. But there was a referral to another cell, and it was his mother's number. Do you want us to investigate that number?"

"Not right now. How about his computer? Any clues there?"

"Just what we reported earlier about grooming sights. He had the regular teen hangouts... school assignments. Nothing unusual."

"Okay. I'll get back with you about the other phone."

Alan wondered why Mona had let Carlos use her phone. He called her. "Mrs. Rivera, did you ever let Carlos use your phone?"

Mona hesitated and then let out a long sigh. "Sometimes. When his father took his phone from him as a punishment, I would let him use mine. I just thought he needed a phone for daily use. Why?"

"We're looking for leads on who he might have been in communication with the weeks before. Can I have your phone number so I can look through the calls?"

Mona gave him her number. Alan sent the number to IT. Next, he called the number Damon had given the officers. The cell had been disconnected. Alan sat back on his chair and stared at the white board. His phone rang.

"Detective Sharp? This is Officer Rosen, sir. I've interviewed several of the stores and places around the vicinity of the murder, and they didn't recognize Carlos Rivera. But they did recognize Alik Leonard and two of the kids he hangs out with. They report that the kids steal from their shops and threaten their employees. I have some CCTV footage of the kids. Do you want me to send it to you?"

"Yes. Thank you. Any idea where they can be found?"

"No... they belong to a gang that refuses to give any information when approached. I guess their threats are frightening enough that no charges are ever posted. They supposedly belong to an even larger network of gangs. People are afraid of what they might do to their families."

"Okay, let's keep on this. Right now, I'm looking for the teen who was around when Carlos was killed. His name is Damon, and he obviously lied about his address and cell number. Ask around and see if anything comes up."

Damon heard a police officer was looking for him. He wasn't about to get involved with the murder of that kid because he already had a record for shoplifting and had been given enough chances. He couldn't go home because the police would eventually find him. He hadn't seen his mother in three weeks anyway and his father was in prison. Everything was going south right now, and his only hope was to leave town and get away from this mess. When some guy in the homeless encampment in Roxbury offered Damon a place to sleep last week, he took it. But that wasn't going to last forever because the guy was getting on his nerves and had even offered him money to be a runner. Damon knew the stories about using kids for trafficking, drug sales and other criminal activity. He wasn't going to go to jail like his father. One way out was to find RJ and then find somewhere to stay off the grid, probably using food kitchens and missions that were always open to street kids with no questions asked. Damon pledged not to join a gang, even when they offered surrogate families and protection from violence and harassment. Right now, Damon needed protection from the gang.

Alan wondered again if Carlos' murder could be gang related and maybe sparked by initiation for membership. Gang initiation had always been tied to mob mentality designed to test loyalty, resilience and nerve. Sometimes initiation involved a violent crime that might include threat, murder, gang-rape or drive-by shootings. Alan knew that years ago when a gang member started a fight it would end only with injuries. Nowadays, kids don't have fighting skills, so they just shoot each other. Unfortunately, the city and state programs have been stretched and can't keep pace with the number of tragedies due to guns. And most kids who carry guns live on the margins of criminal family history, anyway. Sometimes, they don't have a choice. Was Alik Leonard trying to prove himself when he shot Carlos?

Before Alan could organize his thoughts, Vivian was standing at his door.

Alan raised his eyebrows and said, "What is it?"

"Detective Sir, I have a kind of funny feeling about the gun case. I think I recognize Mrs. Murphy from somewhere. I've gone over this in my head and maybe it's from one of the cold cases I had in Hartford."

Alan looked even more amazed. "That's a stretch. Do you remember the case?"

"Well... that's the thing. I have a very good memory for faces, even though this case was years ago. She was younger, and so that's what got me wondering."

"Wondering?"

"If she were involved with an investigation back then, and someone's trying to blackmail her."

Alan took a sip of his coffee. He was surprised by this new information but doubted it was the breakthrough they needed. "What do we know about her?"

"I'd like to take some time and investigate it... if it's okay with you."

"Go ahead. If you need Detective Lane's help, ask her." He then dismissed her, then remembered. "Wait... Please report all that you discover to Captain Johnson."

Vivian was confused. "Why would I do that?"

Alan didn't know if she was refusing or questioning his decision. "Please just do it. That's all."

Vivian almost saluted but checked herself. Sasha had warned her that it wasn't necessary. She backed out of the door.

Alan watched her walk out and wondered, again, if she was the best choice. She seemed nervous and almost intimidated around him. Did he affect others this way? He liked to work closely with his fellow officers because any collaboration fostered a strong sense of camaraderie and teamwork. Everyone worked towards a common goal. Alan also knew that they all faced high levels of stress and pressure to solve cases, which could be mentally and emotionally taxing. And it wasn't like any of them earned a great deal of money for all the hours they put in. Like teachers, medical staff and small business owners, you were never compensated for the extra hours.

Alan called Sasha back to his office to regroup. If Vivian did the legwork on the gun, they could get back to the murder investigation. "Officer Rosen just sent some CCTV coverage of some gang members who are causing trouble in the area Carlos was hanging out. Let's go through it together."

After forty-five minutes of careful viewing, they printed copies of four potential suspects who looked suspicious. Alan sat back in his chair and asked, "I guess it's time to talk with Leonard again. I'm guessing that he knows these teens... but I also guess he won't give them up."

Sasha agreed. "We could use another approach... saying we were concerned that these guys were in danger. If Alik was killed, they may be next."

Alan liked this idea. "Let's run these faces through the system and see what comes up."

A MATTER OF TIME

Later that day, Pierce Leonard sent for his foot soldiers. They were a group of teens who hung around the lobby of the building and were ready to take orders. They were hustlers, selling candy, washing car windows, running messages, or doing jobs that didn't require drug sales because Pierce demanded that they stay clear of drugs. He knew that most of these kids had an addictive behavior problem even before they touched a drink or a drug, and most of their parents were addicts. Pierce was trying to keep them in school and out of trouble.

Eleven teens crowded into the office of the building, sitting on the floor or leaning against the walls. Pierce sat at his desk making eye contact with each one. There were four girls which surprised and pleased him. All were dressed in hooded sweatshirts, baggy jeans, clean sneakers, and some had gold chains hanging around their necks. They ranged in age from 14-18. Pierce wanted to talk with them before things started to explode.

"Now look, people," Pierce began, "we all know what happened to Alik and we're all ready to avenge his death. I get it… I'm angry, too. The police were here to take down any information and I said nothing. I don't know who did this or why. Alik was on his own for a while and I understand he stayed in cars some nights. That's all I know. But somebody beat him to death. Does anybody here know who did this?"

The room was quiet except for a slight shuffling of feet. Finally, a hand went up and a girl asked, "I thought Alik was in trouble for shooting that kid."

Pierce nodded. "You're right. He was questioned. Does anyone know who was with him the day it happened?"

Everyone looked around to see if someone would tell

who they all suspected. The room was silent.

"I need the names of the guys who were with Alik that day. I also need to find out who Alik was hanging out with on the day he died. Someone followed him to the car and beat him to death. Find me the names and I'll take care of them."

Pierce dismissed the group with the warning not to engage in fights or harm anyone because the police were on the lookout. They would take care of things their way.

SATURDAY, OCTOBER 14th

Alan waited until after nine to call Sidney. They both worked on Saturday sometimes to catch up on paperwork. Calling each other with a question or to check in was not unusual and always appreciated. Sidney answered on the third ring. "Alan! How are things?"

Alan smiled into the phone and hoped his friend knew it. "Good morning! Things are okay… busy. How about you?"

"Same. I'm up to my ears in cases and find myself thinking about easing out of the firm. I suppose I could work from home, or better yet work only three days a week."

"Is that an option for you?"

"Yes! Senior lawyers get this option after putting in so many years. I've already called HR to set something going. I'd like to put in more hours volunteering for Carla."

"I'm sure she'd like that. Police retirement here is 65, and I've already got my 20 years in. Since I'm 68, I can get my pensions and social security and be comfortable. But what the devil am I going to do with my time?"

Sidney let out a loud laugh. "We always go back to that same question. You can volunteer…"

"I know." Alan paused before he said, "I'm thinking about being a PI." That was the first time he had ever mentioned it to anyone.

"Really! A private investigator? Put up a shingle?"

"Perhaps. It's just an idea. I could work on cases when I felt like it. Sounds good to me. Anyway, I have a quick question for you. I'm working through all the possible scenarios on a case now, and I'm wondering what you can tell me about property crime."

"You mean like larceny? Breaking and entering?"

"Breaking in and taking property... like a weapon."

Sidney thought for a moment. "Okay, larceny as you know, is taking someone else's property without consent and with the intent to keep. There must be proof of guilt beyond reasonable doubt. So, let's say someone picks a lock and enters but doesn't intend to take anything and leaves immediately... that's not a crime. Home invasions encompass additional factors that elevate it to a more serious crime than mere trespassing. But stealing a weapon... penalties vary depending on the type of weapon. And of course, if it's used in a crime, the perpetrator may face additional charges and penalties. Can you tell me more about this?"

"I have two cases of stolen guns. One has been used in a murder; the other is still at large. What defense might be used against charges of stealing a gun?"

"It could include lack of intent, mistaken identity, or lack of evidence proving who stole the gun."

"That's what I thought. Thanks."

"Let me know how I can help. I heard about the kid who was murdered by the project. Was that Pierce Leonard's relative?"

"Yeah. I hope Leonard doesn't think he has to solve this."

When Alan hung up, he once again thought about his

years on the force. He'd known other guys who returned to part-time work once they retired. They sometimes came back and volunteered as mentors and advisors for new recruits. But the idea of being a PI and having his own business, and setting his own hours, was the most appealing.

Vivian was eager to work on the Murphy case, even though it was the weekend. She wasn't the most organized person according to her last review, so she had bought an Apple Notebook to help her stay focused. Because she was tech smart, she relied on her written notes to bring cases to logical conclusions. This worked with cold cases, and she hoped it would help her now. She also had an uncanny ability to read between the lines, and she had a feeling someone at the Murphy's was hiding something. She decided to pay them a visit.

She arrived at the Murphy house close to 9:30. Because it was the weekend, she didn't call ahead, but hoped Tom and Sheila were home. Sheila opened the door. "Mrs. Murphy, I'm Detective Collins and I'd like to ask you some follow-up questions about the stolen gun."

Sheila looked annoyed. "Have you found it?"

"No, but I've notified several places to keep an eye out for it. May I come in?"

Sheila Murphy crossed her arms and stood firm. "I thought we gave you all the information you needed. What more do you possibly want from us?" Sheila didn't want to carry on a discussion with this detective because she was falling apart and trying to hide her anxiety from everyone. Her issues were both psychological and physical because she worried obsessively about circumstances not in her control and often medicated herself to avoid panic attacks. She tried to discipline herself to avoid emotional outbursts and to constantly remind herself not to overthink everything... to take a moment of reflection. But since their house had been ransacked and a gun had been stolen, she was in panic mode. She invited Vivian in and reluctantly offered coffee which Vivian accepted. As she watched Sheila pour the water into the maker, Vivian asked, "Are you from around here?"

Sheila stopped abruptly from her task and turned toward Vivian. "Why do you ask?"

"Just curious. I'm from Hartford. Have you ever been there?" Vivian kicked herself for being so obvious. "I'm always a little TMI... sorry." But she had seen a moment of caution in Sheila's face. "I grew up on the coast."

Vivian was curious about this vague answer. Sheila didn't mention which city on the coast or give a clue that she went to Yale in New Haven. Why not answer directly?

Sheila brought the steaming cup over to Vivian and asked, "What more do you want to know about the missing gun?"

"Is your husband home? We should probably talk about it when he's present."

Sheila looked at her watch. "He had an early meeting." She took out her phone and pushed a button. Vivian could hear the ringing tone and finally a voice appeared. "Where are you?" Sheila listened and then hung up. "He's on his way."

Vivian met Tom at the door and introduced herself.

Tom looked confused. "Where's my wife?"

Sheila called from the kitchen, "I'm in here. I guess they have more questions for us." She was still angry at her husband for having a gun without telling her.

Just then Caleb rushed into the kitchen. He was holding his laptop and looked confused, "Mom... Dad... do you own a gun?"

Lieutenant Johnson had a game of golf scheduled for the afternoon and considered not answering the call. He noticed the caller ID... it was Sheila. He wanted to ignore it because he didn't feel like listening to his sister-in-law rant about police priorities. But, then again, he felt guilty because she was family. "Hello, Sheila. What's up?"

"Dale... we need to talk with you about this investigation getting out in the media. Caleb's being targeted."

Vivian was speaking with Caleb when Johnson arrived. He quickly greeted Sheila and Tom and then asked Vivian to give him a minute. "What do you know so far?"

"Sir, it appears that Caleb received an anonymous threat on his phone warning him that the gun they found in the house was going to be posted publicly if his parents don't send money."

"How much?"

"Fifty thousand dollars."

"And I'm assuming Caleb doesn't have a clue who sent this to him."

"No, sir. It popped up as a text and was immediately erased."

"Caleb erased it?!"

"No... there's a system available that will erase texts immediately after it's sent."

"So, Caleb didn't reply and there's no way to find out who sent it."

"It appears so, yes." Vivian wanted to explain more to

Johnson but didn't want to insult his position by knowing more about social media than she believed he did.

Johnson called his nephew over. "Caleb, I'll need to take your phone and run it by the tech department. Is that the only anonymous text you've received?"

"Yeah... it spooked me. We're all anti-gun in this family... so now I'm confused." Caleb looked younger than his eighteen years, his hands running through his long hair.

"Can you think of anyone who wants to hurt you or cause trouble? A bully or some angry kid who might have broken into your house?"

"I've thought about it and I don't think any of my friends would do that. I mean... we have some jerks at school, but I've never been targeted."

Johnson was aware that Tom was listening. Being a lawyer, he wanted to protect his son, even though he saw how upset Caleb was getting. "Caleb, let me talk with your uncle now." They watched Caleb leave the room. "And son, please don't let this get out. It's strictly confidential now."

He then looked overcome with worry. "What should we do, Dale? Besides the threat of letting this out, there was a plea for money... what's the next step?"

"Your guess is as good as mine. I'll take the phone and see if I can find the person who sent it. I'm assuming the gun was taken when your house was torn apart. The question is: did they come looking for the gun after all?"

"I'm telling you... nobody knew I had a gun. I haven't even looked at it for years! I've explained this all to Sheila." Sheila touched her temple and closed her eyes. How could this happen to her family?

Johnson wanted to warn Tom. "The other problem is

if the gun's used in a crime. You don't want this to happen. The faster we get it back, the better for everyone."

Vivian was following the conversation and taking notes. Now that the gun was in someone's hands, she didn't need to search for it online. Unless, of course, this is a bluff. She wanted to keep all options open.

Vivian's first call when she left the Murphy home was to Alan. "Yes. Detective Collins, how can I help you?"

"Sir, we have a kind of breakthrough with the Murphy case. It's a bit off the track... meaning not what we thought." Vivian let this idea sink in. "The oldest son, Caleb, just received a threatening text saying someone had the gun and wanted money... Fifty thousand dollars!"

Alan could tell that Vivian was out of breath. She was stringing things together quickly and maybe wanted some sort of guidance. "Did you notify Lieutenant Johnson, Detective?"

"Yes, sir. He arrived at the house immediately and talked with everyone. He advised them to wait while he found out what he could. The Lieutenant took the laptop and phone with him to run it through tech."

Alan thought for a minute. "Did the Murphys call you first?"

Vivian hesitated. She had made the decision herself to learn more about the gun and now wondered if she had overstepped some protocol. "No, sir. I visited the Murphy's this morning to inquire about the gun because I was new to the case. I had put out some feelers to see if it had been sold and maybe hoped for more details."

"Okay... I understand. It's good you were there to hear how things happened. Stay in touch with Johnson and see what he wants you to do."

"Yes, of course." Vivian hung up and thought about working with the Lieutenant. She didn't feel pressure but knew there would be high expectations. She had already heard that he was respected and fair, but his communications skills were lacking. She reminded herself to stay calm, focused and proactive.

Alan heard from Johnson later in the day. He planned to keep Detective Collins on the case because he remembered her computer knowledge. If this was some sort of cyber bullying, she might know how to get to the source.

SUNDAY, OCTOBER 15th

Alan woke up in a mood. His back hurt as he struggled out of bed and limped to the bathroom. He seemed to be falling apart... first his knee and now his back. He reached for some Tylenol and looked at himself in the mirror. He looked like his grandfather! *Not too bad,* he thought, at least he remembered him as a great guy. He had been a sheriff in a small Colorado town. When did he retire from his job?

Alan thought about all the pesky, time-consuming tasks he had each day... scheduling meetings, managing officers... scrolling through all the spam emails that targeted him. He thought about how crime shows depict law enforcement and the legal process in an unrealistic way. From renegade cops who single-handedly take down suspects to crime labs filled with futuristic tech. In fact, most police departments are funded by taxpayers' money, and the budget rarely has enough to keep the department up to date.

Alan was still thinking about this when he went to make coffee. These shows make police work look exciting. And Hollywood stereotypes depict police officers as unemotional machines... but they're human beings who have rules to follow and who protect the very people who might be complaining. Even firing one bullet triggers an extensive investigation into a police officer's actions to determine if any policies or procedures were violated. Alan appreciated how the system worked to protect his officers.

Who was he kidding? He was addicted to work. The option of getting a license for private investigating was on his mind because he liked the idea of having an office that wasn't cluttered with reports and deadlines. He even liked knowing that he wouldn't be bothered with multiple questions from officers who should know the answers by now. That thought led him to frustration as he began to grapple with the unpredictability of most cases.

He decided to spend the rest of the day organizing notes about both investigations. It had been over two weeks since Carlos was murdered. And the two guns were still a mystery.

When his phone rang, it took him a minute to stop ruminating on the cases. It was Maggie. "Hello Alan, I was thinking about you this morning."

Alan lit up at the sound of her voice. They missed seeing each other because of Alan's two cases. "I'm glad to hear that… What are your plans for the rest of the day?"

"I'm going to have a late lunch with a woman I just met. She owns a bed and breakfast in town, and I'd love to see how she runs the place."

"Are you considering opening your own bed and breakfast again?" Alan knew how difficult it had been for Maggie to give up her B&B in Washington. She had run her business for over twenty years, knew everyone in town and welcomed all her guests as if they were long time friends. Was she ready to start all over again?

"No, I'm done with that. Just the business side alone

was getting to be a nightmare. This lady is looking for someone to take over when she's away. I like the idea of occasionally stepping in and enjoying the work. I'll know more after today. How are you doing?"

Alan thought this was as good a time as any to tell her about his idea of retirement. "I was talking to Sidney and finally admitted that I want to retire. I'm getting too old to keep up with all the changes in this job with the technology and new rules coming down from above."

"I understand and completely agree with you. Every time I think about new things like AI, it worries me. Who do you believe anymore?"

"Don't even get me started on AI," Alan laughed. "I hope there'll be regulations soon because I worry about the trustworthiness and accountability in this kind of artificial intelligence."

Maggie agreed. "Tell me, Alan, what would you do with yourself if you retired. Take up golf?"

They both laughed. Alan had played tennis in his younger days but hadn't picked up a racket for years. "Well… I'm thinking about opening a private investigation business."

"Really! How interesting. I remember your friend in upstate New York last year who had her own PI business. This sounds intriguing."

Alan knew that Maggie would find only positive things to say about any adventure he took. "I'm just starting to think about it. One thing I know is that sitting at home doing nothing is not appealing."

They spoke some more about getting together and how fast time seems to be moving. When they hung up the phone, Alan appreciated Maggie even more.

A MATTER OF TIME

Alan went back to his paperwork. He liked solving puzzles and each case was becoming more like a nine-dot problem. Alan had always been amused with this puzzle where people were asked to connect the dots in a 9-dot array using no more than four straight lines and without lifting your pen or pencil from the page. The dots were arranged in a box and people seemed to assume the lines must be drawn within the boundaries of the dots.

Alan learned to let go of that assumption and let the lines extend outside the box. He also knew, psychologically, that the "box" was a metaphor for the unnecessary constraints that you put on yourself that can limit creative problem solving. It can be restrictive and confining.

He used this concept with his officers when they needed to change their perspective on a case or even question their assumptions or rules. If they relied on life experiences to make educated guesses even when faced with ambiguous or partial information, they might push to settle because they just didn't see any alternative. Alan's advice was to do three things: describe the behavior, identify assumptions and break rules if necessary... try something new.

Alan was quick to believe he, too, sometimes did this out of habit. It's because of forming first impressions which can be deadly. He always had to remind himself to be open-minded and adapt to any unexpected situation. What was he missing in these two cases?

MONDAY, OCTOBER 16th

Sasha followed Alan into his office when he arrived. "I had a talk with Jet earlier today. I caught him before he got to school, and he said he didn't know where Damon or RJ were. He says he's tried to get in touch with Damon, but there's no answer. I'm worried that they're hiding from the gangs because of Alik's death."

Alan sat at his desk and looked at the white board. What was he missing? If this was a quid pro quo, then someone who knew or suspected Alik of Carlos' death may have taken revenge. And now there was a possibility of gang members trying to find that person to take their own revenge. "Let's consider all the possibilities again, Sasha. First, if Alik killed Carlos... which we are almost certain happened... Anyone who knew Carlos might have a reason to kill Alik. A likely scenario could be that Alik was running from someone and hiding. From what we know, he was an impulsive teen who could easily threaten others, especially since he had a gun. We need information about his activities outside the project. He was looking for a job, we're told, and skipping school. What was he doing all day? We need to trace his activities."

Sasha agreed. "It looks like Pierce Leonard isn't going to help. How will we find more about Alik?"

A MATTER OF TIME

"I want you to call Officer Rosen and be certain we have all the information he gathered about Alik. Let's also get some CCTV tapes in the area on the days before Carlos was killed, maybe two weeks before. If people don't want to talk to us, we can go through the tapes and see if we notice anything that might help."

Sasha left the office and called Rosen. He let out a loud sigh. "It's difficult to get anyone's help. The store people are too nervous about gang repercussions to speak up. But there's one man who runs a gym and said he knew Alik. Let's go talk with him." They made plans to meet in an hour.

Pierce Leonard watched the two teens who were leaning on the wall of the building. He knew they had been hanging around Alik and may have been with him when he stole the gun from his office. They weren't residents of the building, and Pierce wondered if they also slept in abandoned cars. He decided to find out.

"Hey... you two. I want to ask you something." Pierce tried to appear cordial as he walked quickly to detain them. "You hung out with Alik, didn't you?"

The two teens were taken by surprise. They hadn't seen Pierce approach and didn't see a means of escape without looking guilty. "Yeah... we knew him," one of the teens said.

Pierce used his size to corral the teens into a corner. "Do you know who beat him to death?"

Both teens shook their heads and remained silent.

"Do you know where Alik got the gun he used?"

Again, they shook their heads. This time they tried to get past Pierce, shoving him. But Pierce stuck out his arm to stop them. "I need some answers from you two. I know you hung out with my nephew and were probably with him when that kid was shot. I can turn you into the cops, or you can tell me who Alik was afraid of."

Both teens stopped pushing. The tallest one spoke. "He had a lot of enemies 'cause he kept threatening people with the gun. He stole from kids on the street and in stores... he was crazy."

Pierce looked at the other kid. "Where did he do this? Around here?"

The kid looked scared. "Mainly in parking lots and bars after hours. Especially people who were drunk and were easy hits. He just had to show his gun and people handed over cash or whatever they had."

Pierce shook his head slowly. "Did you ever hear that someone was going after him? Stalking him?"

"Yeah... we all heard his name was out there."

Pierce let them go and needed time to process this information. Anyone could have gone after Alik.

Sasha returned to Alan's office. "I spoke with Officer Rosen, and he wants to help. He has contacts in the area and hopes to get some information on the gang activity. He thinks that Alik was a wild card who hung around older gang members. These guys were serious about loyalty and initiation. Maybe that's why Alik had a gun."

"Did Rosen have a name for the gang or members?"

"That's what his contacts might be able to give him. In the meantime, he heard that Pierce Leonard has his own teen soldiers out looking for who did this."

Alan shook his head. "I suspected as much. Leonard seems to hold significant control over all the operations of the group including their movements, plans and actions...

possibly even violent behavior."

Sasha looked concerned. "We'll keep our eyes on alert, sir. Officer Rosen has the name of a gym where Alik hung out and we're going now to ask around. I'll report back."

The gym was in a business district near Roxbury. The front of the building was glass, and passers-by could see bikes, treadmills, and weights being used by members. Sasha and Rosen had called ahead to speak with the manager, Jim Edgewood.

Rosen began the questioning. "We've been told that Alik Leonard was a member of this gym. Did you know him?"

Edgewood nodded. "Yeah. I heard he's been killed. What happened?"

"We're investigating that. How often did he use the gym?"

"It's hard to know. Everyone's supposed to sign in, but Alik didn't. I think he was using the gym to take showers and clean up."

"Who did he hang out with?"

"No one. He came alone and then he left. I asked around the other day about him and no one had a clue. But, then again, this isn't a social club... you exercise and then leave."

"Did he have a locker?"

"Yeah. We cleaned it out and we're going to send it to his address. Do you want it?"

Sasha and Rosen both nodded. Edgewood brought a well-used box with several things packed inside. "You can take it... hope this helps."

Rosen wrote out a receipt for the items. When they got to their car, Rosen asked, "So now what? Do we go through the stuff or take it Detective Sharp?"

Sasha suggested taking it back to the precinct and itemizing the contents.

Later that day, Alan called Vivian in to hear any changes on the Murphy case. "What do we know so far? Any more contact?"

"No, sir. But I'm waiting to see how Lieutenant Johnson wants to proceed. I've got some ideas of my own, but I'll keep them to myself."

Alan looked at her, trying to keep any negative thoughts out of his voice. "Preemptive problem-solving wastes precious time and energy. I believe you are perfectly capable of solving a case. Tell me what you plan to do next."

Vivian lowered her gaze to consider her answer. He was right, she was guessing her way through the investigation and might be causing more work for the department. "Sir, I did a background check on Caleb and found a misdemeanor that was buried." Vivian paused to get Alan's reaction.

"Go on…"

"Although it was a minor offense, a conviction of theft, it might influence his perception of this case. I'm wondering if Caleb suspects someone of stealing the gun… now that he knows about it."

He sat and looked at her. "He didn't know his father even had a gun. So now he wants to find out who took it. That's a stretch, Detective. Besides looking up his record, what other evidence can you point out that involves Caleb?"

Vivian didn't react to Alan's obvious resistance to using her tech skills. She would be surprised if he even had a personal email account. "I'd like to look through Caleb's personal accounts, his Instagram, and social media sites.

Sometimes we find hints of bullying or transgressions that might be attributed to bad choices. I would hate to see him get involved with any of that."

Alan nodded slightly. "Run that by the Lieutenant if you find anything."

Vivian stood for a minute and then realized their discussion was over. She carefully backed out of the room.

Alan wondered if this new generation of officers used their phones too much to solve crimes. He depended on his tech team to handle all the computer evidence and any other important information on a case. They were the experts. The other day he was waiting for his order at a restaurant and noticed that every patron was on their phone. It has become an addiction! Maybe he had professional reasons to stay offline... a privacy thing. Or maybe it was like those video games kids were into... once you get started, it's hard to quit.

TUESDAY, OCTOBER 17th

It had been almost two weeks since Carlos had been gunned down. Because Alik Leonard was the suspect, and now dead, Alan was conflicted. Did the two deaths have the same motive? Initiation or revenge? If this continued to be gang related, then Alan needed to find out more about the street violence in the area. He motioned for Sasha to come to his office.

"Was there any trace of drugs in Carlos' system?"

"No, he was clean. We asked around about his drug use and everyone agreed he didn't do drugs. What are you thinking?"

"I'm looking for a motive in both murders. If we assume that Alik Leonard shot Carlos because of some initiation rule, then we just need to focus on who killed Alik. But... this is a long shot... what if Carlos was really a target? We've completely stopped looking at that as a possibility."

"You mean that Carlos might have been stalking Alik? Or maybe had something on him? If that's true, then maybe he confided in someone about it?"

"That's what I'm thinking... someone else might have known about this and then attacked Alik. We need to investigate this possibility. I think we also need to look up past cases of assaults like this that have gone unsolved."

Sasha nodded. "If Alik used the gun to threaten people and steal from them, Carlos may have known someone who he attacked. Do you think a kid like Carlos would try to approach someone as hostile as Alik?"

"Hard to say. It's just another possibility we need to explore. Right now, we're out of answers for why Alik was killed. My first reaction, of course, has been revenge, but maybe we need to look at something else."

"Officer Rosen and I retrieved a box of items from Alik's gym locker. We've gone through it and there doesn't seem to be anything other than a change of clothes and some photos. Would you like to look?" Alan nodded.

The photos were of Alik and his grandmother. However, in one photo there was a younger woman who may be his mother. Alan remembered that Alik's mother was in prison. "Let's go talk with Valentine Leonard and see what she has to say."

Val was in a medium security prison. Even though some inmates posed a risk, most demonstrated a willingness to comply with institutional rules and regulations. The prison offered job and program opportunities at any level to help prisoners continue their education. Val had taken advantage of these programs and hoped to secure a good job when she got out in thirteen months. She hadn't heard Alik had been killed.

Alan and Sasha parked their car near the entrance of the building and displayed their badges at the door. They had called ahead to have Val waiting in an interview room. She was a full-figured woman who filled out the ill-fitting beige prison jumpsuit to bursting. Her hair was short and beginning to gray, and there were several tattoos visible on her hands.

She appeared to be annoyed. "What's this about?"

Alan introduced himself and Sasha and then made their way to the metal chairs facing Val. "Ms. Leonard, we're here about your son, Alik. Have you heard that he has been killed?"

Val stared at him and then slammed her fist on the table. "What? You're wrong! Alik lives with his grandmother and is safe! Why are you telling me he's dead?"

Sasha reached out to try and calm her, but Val stood up and demanded to be taken back to her cell. Sasha stopped her. "I'm sorry you didn't know this. Can we get you something to drink?"

Val looked at the door to find the guard waiting outside. She held her breath to control her emotions as her brain tried to handle the terrible news. Shaking her head, she slumped back into the chair and began to cry. "What happened? How could someone kill my boy?"

Sasha stood and knocked on the door, asking the guard to bring in some water. Then she went over to Val and put her arms around her shoulder. "This is terrible news. I'm so sorry."

Alan watched and appreciated the care that Sasha showed. They were here for some answers, but it would take some careful questioning to get them. After a bottle of water was given to Val, Sasha sat back down and quietly began the interview. "Ms. Leonard... May I call you Val?"

Val nodded, while taking a long drink of water.

"We're interested in finding the teens who were close to Alik. His friends. So far, no one has come forward to give us information. Do you have a name or names?"

"Didn't you ask Pierce? He would know."

"We did. He didn't give us any names. We also spoke with your mother, and she didn't know either. We've heard that Alik had been hanging around older guys. Did he talk with you about this?"

Val shook her head. "I've been here for over a year, and he's only been to see me twice. I asked him to stay away because this is no place I wanted him to remember." Tears began rolling down her face once more. "Alik was a good kid... just moved around a lot and had a tough time focusing. His teachers said he had a behavior problem because of that. But he was good at math... he loved it." She wiped her tears and looked down at the table. "He didn't deserve to die."

Alan finally spoke up. "I'm sure he didn't. Unfortunately, Alik had a gun and was involved in shooting another boy. Did you know about this?"

Val looked surprised. "No... he wouldn't! How did he get a gun?"

"We believe he stole it. Did you know if Alik took any drugs?"

"Yeah... he took some street stuff off and on. I told him to knock it off because he'd get hooked... like I did. But I suspect as soon as I got caught, he didn't care if he was clean or not."

Alan continued to question. "Do you know who his dealer was?"

Val's eyes darted back and forth to the detectives. "You're kidding... right? You want me to snitch on a drug dealer while I'm in prison? I'm trying to stay clean myself."

Alan nodded. "I understand. Maybe you know where he bought the drugs."

"Pierce is adamant that the teens don't do drugs. But

some of them get away with it. I'd ask a few of the guys who hang around the building what they know about dealers."

The detectives thanked Val and offered to let her know when Alik's funeral would take place. When they got to their car, Sasha said, "That was heartbreaking. I thought she would have been informed about her son's death."

Alan nodded. "Sometimes news like that gets stuck in the system. She should have had a counselor tell her. I'm sorry we were the ones. You were very good with her. Thank you."

By the time they returned to the precinct, they had a new issue to follow up on. Alan wanted to pursue any evidence or proof that led to Alik's dependency on using drugs. It was a common belief that all gang members were involved in drug trafficking, distribution and sales. Alan knew that studies revealed that gang members who bought or sold drugs kept the profit and high-end drugs for themselves. New members, especially young teens, were instructed not to deal or take drugs if they wanted to be included in a gang, but there was apparently an underground dealing that took place among this group.

"Let's assume that Alik was dealing on the side, which meant he was probably using too. If he did have anxiety issues like his mother said, maybe the drugs were to control the impulses or help steady his nerves. Once it got into his system, he probably needed more as the relief abated because of steady use. If that's the case, we have street informants who may be able to lead us to his suppliers. Let's talk with Officer Rosen again and get him on this."

Officer Rosen was waiting at the precinct when Alan and Sasha returned. "I've got some names of dealers in the Roxbury neighborhood who might talk to me. Word is out about the two teens being murdered and everyone is worried about losing their clients. It seems Pierce's apartment building is a good location for sales because it's so close to the freeway. You know, get off, buy, get right back on. People like convenience when they're addicted."

Alan slowly nodded. "What do you think about Carlos being a target? Maybe as some kind of initiation rite. We spoke with Alik's mother, and she indicated he took anti-anxiety drugs because of his impulsive nature. From my understanding, impulsive aggression as opposed to normal forms of aggression can lead to rationalizing violence and the consequences can lead to criminal assault or even murder. Let's say he was on something like Oxycontin which might contribute to his hostility or fear and bring on exaggerated aggressive behavior. Sad as it is, if Alik wasn't diagnosed in school or in any system and given treatment, he might not have been able to control his aggression."

Rosen thought for a minute. "Why was Carlos shot then? Because Alik couldn't control himself?"

"Well, it's a possibility. We need to speak with Alik's teachers and see if this pattern is consistent. Schools are supposed to monitor behavior and offer help... let's see if anyone did."

Sasha offered to go to the schools and Rosen would go to talk with the dealers. They would meet back in the morning.

Alan called Carla. "Are you in the middle of something?" he asked his friend.

"Not right now, Alan. How can I help?" She knew that he only called during office hours for advice or a favor.

"We're still on the case of the teen murders and I

wondered about something. How do teens handle impulsivity? How early does it manifest itself in a child?"

Carla thought for a minute and then began. "Sometimes early life stressors, such as abuse or neglect, can be associated with impulsivity. And experiencing stressors during childhood might lead to substance abuse, ADHD or even bipolar disorder. In teens, we sometimes deal with intermittent explosive disorder, which is the sudden outburst of anger or violence. Is that what you wanted to know?"

"And if it goes untreated?"

"Well, you know the consequences. Our prisons are full of people who need medication to treat their stressors. Who are we talking about... If I may ask."

"The teen who was killed in his car... beaten to death. It seems he had some impulse control issues that might have caused the death of Carlos Rivera."

"Did the boys know each other?"

"Yes. I guess Carlos looked up to Alik. I'm just following this up now. We've been getting nowhere in the two cases and now might need to go another direction."

"Well, Alan, I know you'll figure it all out. I'll keep my ears open for anything I hear from my teens. So far, I've heard nothing."

The two friends spoke a few minutes longer and then promised to get coffee soon.

Alan sat back and considered all the possibilities. If Alik shot Carlos on impulse, who beat him to death? Someone who knew Carlos... or someone who was after Alik. It was time to find out.

Tom and Sheila Murphy believed the police were on their case, but they were not in agreement about what to say to Caleb. Sheila wanted to protect Caleb and Tom wanted to interrogate him.

These were typical responses when dealing with any crisis in their marriage. Sheila stonewalled conversation and Tom overworked an issue to the point of losing focus. Tom always felt there was something that happened in Sheila's life that made her refuse to talk when things got complicated. Maybe it was time to seek a counselor's help and bring this out in the open.

Tom found Sheila in the living room, staring out the window. He sat down on the sofa next to her and said, "Sheila, I want you to consider going with me to a counselor. I think we need to clear the air."

Sheila stared back at her husband. "No... we're fine."

"Then I guess I'll go by myself. I'm feeling stuck. I seem to spend a lot of time trying to manage your refusal to communicate, and I'm wondering if you're holding something back. I think maybe therapy can help to clarify some issues."

Sheila shrank back from him and sat further away. "What are you talking about? What issue?"

"Your sister told me about the roommate you had in college. How she disappeared and how traumatic it was for you. Something like that can trigger anxiety and nervousness in later years. Is that something we need to talk about?"

Sheila started rubbing her arms as if chilled. "That was so long ago... I've dismissed it altogether."

Tom pressed even further. "Was that girl ever found?"

Sheila shook her head and whispered. "I have no idea."

Tom wanted to help her but also needed answers. "But don't you care? Maybe the case has been solved, and you might find some relief that it's finally over."

Just then the doorbell rang. Tom went to the door and opened it to find Vivian there. He was already feeling flustered but took a sharp breath and stepped back. "Detective, please come in." He escorted Vivian into the living room where Sheila sat and refused to get up. "Now what do you want?" she asked harshly.

"Actually, Mrs. Murphy, I'd like to have a private minute with you."

Tom looked at both women and then nodded as he walked out of the room. Vivian waited a moment and then selected an armchair next to the sofa. Not wanting to mince words, Vivian spoke directly and to the point. "Mrs. Murphy, I worked on cold cases for a couple of years in Hartford, and I remember a case of a Yale coed who disappeared in the 90s. Your name came up in the investigation... I know she was your roommate." Vivian paused and looked steadily at Sheila to make certain she was listening. "I just got word that the case has been solved. Some guy confessed and took the police to the body. They found out he'd been involved with several coed slayings." Vivian leaned closer to Sheila and said quietly, "It seems that with all this going on with your family right now, you may feel a bit of anxiety because of this past case. I thought I would let you know it's been solved."

Sheila Murphy sat rigidly and then burst into tears. "Thank you. Thank you."

Vivian nodded and wondered what to do next. "Can I call your husband for you?"

Sheila looked up through her tears and said, "No, I'll talk with him later."

Vivian left the house, hoping she had helped.

WEDNESDAY, OCTOBER 18th

Rosen had spent a good part of the late afternoon trying to track down the dealers who sold to Alik. His contacts were skeptical and refused to help, saying they had lost track of Alik months ago. Rosen knew that most dealers met buyers in a public place to minimize the risk of being assaulted which might account for Alik's movements on the CCTV. He also knew that sellers operating outside the law were uninterested in customers' welfare, addictions or any harm related to using the drug. This resulted in customers falling out of touch with dealers and having to find new contacts. Nobody was talking when a buyer like Alik died because everyone involved only cared about the drugs.

Sasha entered the high school hoping to find more information about Alik. The principal greeted her and escorted her into his office. "I'm sorry to hear about Alik Leonard. He was a troubled boy, but I always hoped he would get his life together and find a new path. How can I help you?"

"Did Alik get in trouble for drugs at school?"

The principal nodded. "Yes. We found he was selling to the middle school kids next door and turned him in to the authorities. You probably have his record... but it may be sealed because he was a minor."

"We're aware of his drug dealing. Can you give me the

names of anyone who sold with him? We're looking for dealers."

"I wish I could help. I've asked our teachers and all staff to keep watch for any activity that looks like or promotes drug dealing or selling. We have a strict policy about drugs, and it includes suspension and treatment. We also have rules about confidentiality and so I can't give you names."

"How about students who Alik hung out with?"

"I wrote down a couple of student's names." He handed a paper to Shasha. "I'm not certain how much they hung out after school, though."

Sasha understood that these names were the best she could get from the principal. Protecting students in his care was number one on his list of duties and implicating anyone in a criminal act would never happen. Sasha thanked him.

Alan was frustrated when he listened to Rosen and Sasha relate their findings. Not having sufficient witnesses or hard evidence continued to plague these cases. He told them to write up their reports and that he was going to pay another visit to Pierce Leonard.

Alan looked at his watch and realized the day had gotten away from him and traffic would be a mess due to all the commuters. As he climbed into his car he thought of all the complaints about traffic from citizens who thought the police should do something about it. But no awareness of using local transportation or carpooling had deterred people from driving their own vehicles into the city. As a result, rush hour seemed to last all day, becoming like other parts of the country where Alan knew it was reported to be even worse... LA and Seattle. He pulled out into traffic and decided not to get uptight about missing lights and crawling along. He knew that other drivers were just as frustrated, and out of habit he automatically turned to the driver next to him. Apparently, this guy had no problem waiting for cars to move because he had his window down, was smoking a cigarette and seemed to be enjoying some loud music that Alan could barely make out. The man must have sensed someone was looking his way, because he glanced quickly through Alan's closed window and then tried to inch his truck forward.

Alan thought for a moment and then looked again at the man's profile before his car moved along. He knew that guy. He was the guy at the hospital... Edgar Rivera's boss at the car place. Alan remembered how upset he'd been when he talked to him on the phone about Carlos being shot. Edgar had spoken about his boss with loyalty, but also with some trepidation. Did this guy have an aggressive side that might get out of control? Could he be someone who wanted to take matters into his own hands? Is it possible that someone close to the Riveras like this guy was involved with Alik's murder? Even if all he did was provide support or assistance or encourage someone else to go ahead and commit the crime, he would be guilty.

Alan knew he was probably grasping at straws, making a desperate attempt to find a solution. He pulled his car over and phoned Sasha to do a background check on Miquel Juarez. Alan wanted to check every angle... every box.

Pierce had spent the morning with Ella. She seemed overwhelmed with grief and at a loss of what to do or say. He didn't tell her that Alik had stolen his gun and used it to scare people because he was feeling troubled for keeping a gun accessible, even when he thought it was safely hidden. If she knew that Alik might have killed that boy, and then died because of it, Pierce wondered if she might turn her grief into anger and demand some consequences. Although it wasn't his job to find Alik's killer, he knew everyone in the building expected him to seek justice.

Pierce had instructed his foot soldiers to find and bring in the person who killed Alik. What would he do if they caught this guy? Turn him in? Watch the legal system spend days and weeks protecting this criminal? That would be the path of least resistance and what the law demanded. But Pierce knew it would take an act of bravery for him to deny retaliation for Alik's death when everyone in the building wanted revenge. On the other hand, he didn't plan on going to jail if he failed to follow the law. A sense of overwhelming powerlessness hit him as he walked through the lobby to his office.

"Mr. Leonard?"

Pierce turned and saw Detective Sharp heading his way. "Do you have a minute?"

Shaking his head slowly, he hoped he communicated to Alan that he didn't have time. "I'm busy."

Alan persisted. "I only have a few questions. Please, let me ask them and then I'll leave."

Pierce shook his head again and then led Alan into the tiny office. "What do you need?" he asked cautiously. He left Alan standing and went around his small desk to sit.

"I heard you were looking for your nephew's killer. I am cautioning you not to get involved. We have people working on the case. Have you spoken to your sister, Valentine?

Pierce looked surprised. "No. We don't speak at all."

"I went to see her at the prison. She didn't know what

happened to Alik, and she was very upset. She told me he took drugs a while ago to curb his anxiety and she hoped he wasn't still on them. Do you know about this?"

Pierce looked down at his hands, trying to protect any knowledge he had about Alik. "I'm not certain he took drugs, Detective."

"We're looking for his dealer. Can you help us?"

"I cannot." Pierce stood up to indicate he was not answering more questions.

Alan turned to go but stopped to warn Pierce. "Please don't get involved. We'll find the murderer so you can help your community to heal."

Alan walked away and questioned if Pierce was brave enough to face the consequences if he got involved. Pragmatism was called for now and was more important than moralism, or revenge. At its core, revenge was only an attempt to regain a sense of control, or in some cases, seek justice. Alan knew that revenge might offer a momentary sense of satisfaction, but it often led to more retaliation and could cause further conflict. Pierce didn't seem like the kind of person to break the law.

Alan returned to the precinct to wait for Sasha and Rosen and go over their reports. He was feeling exhausted and seemed completely depleted of energy. Lately, he couldn't seem to fall asleep at night as his mind drifted through hours of reviewing his cases. He hated all the advice people gave about getting up if you can't sleep and doing something constructive or keeping a sleep diary. The last thing he wanted to do was get up and probably stay up. He usually just tossed around until he finally got a few hours' sleep.

Struggling to keep his eyes open, Alan decided to

close his office door and try to take a short nap on the sofa Maggie insisted he get for his office. It was surprisingly comfortable, and she had even put pillows and a warm blanket... stylish and indiscreet ... on the arms. His plan was to rest and then take a few laps around the outer office to check on his officers.

As he drifted off, he thought about the murders. Both families were suffering the acute pain of grief. Alan knew there was no timetable for the feelings of pain and loss, nor was it possible to avoid suffering. For some people grief lasts a short time, and for others it can be prolonged, even years. What Alan saw in Edgar and Pierce was anger; anger that could linger and get them into trouble. This worried him.

Thirty minutes later Alan was awoken by a knock on his door. He quickly sat up and ran his hands over his face. Shaking his head a couple times, he walked to the door and met Sasha, who was holding a report. "Alan, I have a background check on Juarez. You'll want to see this."

Alan invited her in, offered her a chair and sat at his desk to review the information. Juarez had been picked up several times for assault. He was never charged because the victims refused to press charges. Alan decided quickly, "Let's go talk to him."

The Juarez auto shop looked like a regular place for defective machinery and vehicles to be maintained and repaired. It was a spacious garage equipped with vehicle lifts, diagnostic machines, hand tools, and parts. The shop's responsibilities included maintaining accurate records, performing regular maintenance repairs and updating technical skills.

Alan and Sasha entered the run-down building

through the giant garage door. Several vehicles were on the lifts and at least five workers were inspecting or repairing several cars. Alan walked up to the person closest to the door and asked to speak with Juarez.

"He's out," said the man without a glance in Alan's direction.

"When will he return?"

"Who knows?" The man kept his eyes on the car.

"Is there someone else in charge at the moment?"

"Nope."

Alan became frustrated and nodded to Sasha and then towards an office door. She casually walked through the open door and sat at the desk. There she found a business card for Juarez and something else... Rivera's phone number, along with a photo of Juarez and the Rivera family having dinner on the beach. That wouldn't have been unusual, but she also noticed Mona's phone number on a slip of paper, and it was underlined several times.

After recording the photo and note on her cell, she quickly exited the office and raised her eyebrows at Alan, acknowledging that she needed to talk with him. When they left the garage, she pointed out her concerns that maybe Mona and Juarez were up to something.

Alan looked surprised at that idea. "Now... that's a real stretch! He probably kept the number on his desk to remember to make regular calls to the family."

Sasha shook her head slightly. "I think we better keep every possibility open at this point. We know that murder takes away the feeling of safety and feels profoundly unfair, and leaves the family as victim's, too. Mona and Edgar will never know Carlos's final moments and must guess at what really happened. They will never make sense of it but are consumed to know the truth. What if Mona expressed so much anger and grief that Juarez thought it was his duty to take revenge?"

There it was again... revenge. Alan thought Sasha might be onto something. "I suppose that could be the case. And you're right, Sasha, we can't dispute the fact that Juarez has a stake in this, too, since they're all good friends. Let's send someone to pick up Juarez when he gets back to work." Once again, Alan was impressed with Sasha's quick and ready insight.

Miguel Juarez was worried. Did that detective know who he was? When he stared at him on the road, Miguel had a gut-wrenching feeling that he had to get out of town. He had been in trouble before and didn't want to take any chances. He needed to keep driving. Laying low for a few days might get him off the police radar.

THURSDAY, OCTOBER 19th

The first thing Alan thought when he woke up was the expression his mother often used when things just didn't seem right. *"There's a fly in the ointment,"* she would say. Then she would talk about a condition that was almost too pleasing, when there was something hidden or unexpected... a source of annoyance... an irritating flaw. Alan needed to consider the unexpected now in both investigations.

This bothered Alan all the way to work. He looked quickly at the time and decided it was early enough to see if Sidney was at his office.

"Alan... what's up?" Sidney looked at his watch and saw it was only eight. Alan was usually early to work, so it must be an investigation question.

"Well," Alan began, "you know the expression there's a fly in the ointment?"

"Sure. Like some small and irritating flaw that spoils the whole. What's the problem?"

"I can't get a good hold on my investigation of the murders of the two teens. I know now that one teen killed the younger one and was then found dead in an abandoned car three days later, but it seems almost too easy to assume it's related. I think there's something wrong, hidden, or unexpected somewhere."

Sidney understood. "You know when an investigation stalls it can be due to lack of actionable information, a lack of new leads or in my case as a lawyer, the expiration of the statute of limitations. But I suppose from your point of view, it's because witnesses are hard to find, or no one will speak up for fear of retaliation. It's about the gang… right?"

"Yes. Everywhere we look and everyone we speak to refuses to answer our questions. I believe the neighborhood is frightened or threatened to persuade them to keep quiet. It's all about coercing people through threats of violence."

"So, you think a gang is creating a sense of urgency and dependence through fearmongering and maybe offering protection for people to go along with them."

"Well, let's go back to intimidation. Gangs often use it to enforce compliance through various means, such as aggressive conduct, verbal threats and demonstrations of authority. They exert control this way. I just wish someone would own up to being used this way so we can get a clear picture of who's doing it."

"How can I help, Alan?"

"I need you to look up who owns the building in the project we're investigating. I'm getting nowhere trying to find this out. Maybe there's a link to an organization behind all this subterfuge that will give me a clue."

"I'll get right on it." Sidney hung up and began his search.

Vivian waited until Alan was off the phone before she knocked on his door. "Sir, can I talk with you for a moment?" She walked into the office and sat down on the chair beside his desk.

Alan was taken aback. What now? "What do you need, Detective?"

Vivian took out her laptop and opened it up. Alan thought she was talking to herself, because she was mumbling something and looking intently at the screen as if carrying on a conversation. She suddenly looked up and said, "I've been thinking about the missing gun at the Murphys and think I might have found a solution to the case." She finally settled on a site and turned her computer around to Alan. "I've been browsing through Caleb Murphy's phone and found some hidden messages in a special folder called unknown senders. It looks like Caleb might have had contact with someone unknown and tried to misdirect it... or keep it off record... which was smart." Vivian looked up at Alan as if asking permission to continue.

"Go on," Alan said.

She showed Alan an example. "You see, you can hide messages behind grey blocks and have the text automatically deleted once it's read. It appears that Caleb tried to hide unwanted messages to keep select personal matters private."

Alan interrupted her, "I know about the invisible ink that turns your text into blurry spots in five seconds or so... what does this all have to do with Murphy's case?"

Vivian sat back and closed her laptop. "Caleb was smart, but so are hackers. He may not have been aware that he was giving personal information to someone disguised as another user his age. If he mentioned that the family was going away for a while, it would be an excellent opportunity for a burglary."

"Isn't he the oldest? You would think he'd be aware of privacy and confidentiality when it comes to texting."

"That's true, sir. But once people get used to using sites like this, they believe everyone is on their side. They can complain about school, parents, classmates, and know it won't be saved. The problem is that it's information the stalkers are looking for."

"How did they know where he lived?"

"Good question. These criminals are very clever. They look for clues and can then figure out locations. It's a game to them."

"So, you think Caleb led them to his house and they found the gun. Why didn't they take anything else of value?"

"Maybe when they found the gun and the papers, they knew they had some leverage to extort."

"What will you do now?"

"I'm going to talk with Caleb. Lieutenant Johnson has given me the okay to move on what I find, but I wanted to run this by you before I proceed."

Alan thought for a moment. "I suggest you go easy on the kid. Don't accuse him of anything because his father will come down hard on our unit."

Vivian stood and nodded eagerly. "Of course. Thank you, sir."

Alan watched her walk out of his office and hoped she was right about Johnson giving the okay. Family matters were always tricky.

When Alan's phone rang, he was surprised to see it was Sidney. "That was fast!" he remarked.

Sidney let out a quick laugh. "It was easier to find the information than I thought. That building project is one of the oldest low-income developments around. Over the years, it's had a reputation for being a seriously rough place to live.

Since rent is subsidized, you need to be a special kind of needy, or broke, to live there. But don't get me wrong, apparently since Pierce Leonard took over as manager, the building has improved."

Alan quickly asked, "Who owns it?"

"It varies with these projects. Private equity firms rank among the largest owners, but the federal government or Housing Authority subsidizes many projects. The one you asked about is owned and operated by the feds. That's why Leonard is slowly getting it back on its feet... he's applied to get funds for improvement."

Alan nodded into the phone. "Good to know. I'm liking that guy... just hope he doesn't get into trouble trying to track down who killed his nephew. Thanks for this information."

"Glad to help."

Alan looked at his watch. It was already eleven and he hadn't made any progress on either case. When he looked up, Sasha was at his door with coffee and a bag of sandwiches. She handed him the receipt and sat beside his desk. "You really don't have to do this... but thank you. I'm glad you're here because I'm needing to break things down again, decide what to do... and have lunch." He smiled across at her.

"I thought so. Let's take a minute to talk about the case Detective Collins is working on. She's asked me about it, but I don't have any real knowledge about what's going on."

Alan took a sandwich out of the bag and opened it. His favorite, chicken salad. "It involves a burglary or Beacon Hill and the only item stolen was a gun and some paperwork. Tom Murphy is the owner of the gun and doesn't want his name publicized because he's an anti-gun activist. The oldest boy in the family, Caleb, just got a text from someone saying they would take the gun to the media if they didn't get paid. That's about it."

Sasha slowly opened her sandwich packaging and took a bite. Shaking her head for a moment she asked, "Why did we get the case? Burglaries like this don't usually fall in our jurisdiction."

Alan smirked. "Mrs. Murphy is Lieutenant Johnson' s sister-in-law. She wants this to go away."

Sasha raised her eyebrows. "Does Vivian know that?"

Alan nodded. "She's working on a theory that Caleb has been cyberstalked and that's why this happened. I think she might be on to something."

Sasha took a sip of coffee. "What's next on the teen murders?"

"We need to find Miguel Juarez."

Vivian was on her way to speak with Caleb at school. Because he was eighteen, he was free to talk with her without his parents. The principal was concerned when she called ahead to request a meeting, but she reassured him it was only procedure and that Caleb was not in trouble.

Caleb walked into a conference room of the school and stopped at the door. "What do you want?"

Vivian stood up and asked him to have a seat. "I just have a few questions about your phone text. You're not in trouble, but I assumed you didn't want your parents to know about some of the sites you visit."

Caleb stared at her before he sat down on a comfortable office chair. "What are you talking about... what texts?"

Vivian took out a printed copy of the texts she had

located, indicating that they had been recovered from iCloud. "Do these look familiar?"

Caleb looked stunned. "How did you get these?"

"Caleb, the reason I'm concerned is because I think you might have unknowingly led some criminal to your house and that's why you found out about the missing gun."

Caleb sat back in his chair and shook his head repeatedly. "They were all my friends. You think one of them has my dad's gun?"

"No, probably not. I think someone was setting you up… someone you didn't know. It happens on these sites that criminals will hack in and glean information. For instance, if you said your family was going away, they would try to listen for your location… ask questions that seemed mildly annoying or confusing at first but that leads to your address. I know this sounds crazy, but hackers are getting better at that."

"What do you want me to do?"

"Get a new phone. Only give the number to those you trust. You know the drill, Caleb. Be aware that these sites are not reliable."

"Are you going to tell my parents about all this?"

"I will make a report to them and include this information. I'm not pointing fingers, just the facts we need to find the gun."

The school bell rang, and Caleb stood to go to class. He turned at the door and said, "Thanks."

Vivian liked Caleb. He wasn't like the entitled teens she dealt with who ignored adults or thought they deserved special treatment or recognition for things they didn't earn. Her daughter constantly complained about elite teens who believed the world owed them without ever giving back in return. Unfortunately for teens with egotistical behavior, life can be filled with disappointment, loneliness and isolation because they don't know how to meet their own needs. Vivian thought about Sadie and all the trouble she had in Hartford with girls who were not her friends.

That morning, they had had words about Sadie's grades and how she'd be grounded for the weekend if she didn't hand in her assignments. Vivian decided to call Sadie to make certain she was online with her school assignments and to test her attitude. When Sadie didn't answer, Vivian reminded herself to keep a positive mindset and not to panic, because that might cloud her judgment. She took a minute to think through each step of this morning's conversations. Sadie had stormed out of the room saying she wanted to go live with her father, which was never an option.

Vivian took a detour before driving back to the precinct to check in on Sadie. When she opened the basement door, she heard swearing coming from the kitchen. Sadie was trying to clean up the stove from an explosion of what looked like eggs and pancake mix spread all over the room.

Vivi held her breath. Her daughter was safe.

Alan and Sasha tried to reach Juarez by calling the Riveras, but they hadn't heard from Miguel. When they tried the auto shop, the phone rang several times and then went to voicemail. Alan decided to try a different route. "Did you find any relatives for Juarez in the area when you did the background check?"

Sasha looked over the report. "The only one is a brother in Springfield. Should we contact him to see if Miguel's with him?"

"Let me call the police chief in the city. I know him

from another case, and he could send someone over to check."

Police Chief Martin remembered Alan. "Good to hear from you. What's the deal with this guy?"

"He might be involved with a case we're following. If he's aiding and abetting or even providing support or assistance to someone else, we need to talk with him."

"Are you referring to the two murder cases of the teens?"

"Yes. But right now, I just need to find Juarez. Could you send a car over and see if he's at this address?"

"Sure thing. Do you want us to take him in for questioning?"

Alan thought for a minute. If Juarez was involved and hiding, Alan would have him transported back to Boston. "Yes. Contact me as soon as you can... I'll send someone to meet him at your station." Boston to Springfield was ninety minutes away.

Miguel sat on the front step of his brother's house having a smoke when the police car drove up. He started to run, but a young officer accompanying the chief chased him down.

One hour later, Juarez was on the way back to Boston. He wanted a lawyer and so Alan got a warrant to search Miguel's car and shop. If he needed a lawyer, he was guilty of something.

Sasha tried to call Mona to ask about the note she found on Miguel's desk. If she was in contact with him, she might be aware of his intention for causing harm to Alik. Mona wasn't home. Sasha left a voice message.

Mona was feeling numb and trying to get through

each day. It wasn't just grief, it was trauma. The shock of losing Carlos in such an unexpected and horrible manner had caused her to have disturbing mental thoughts that seemed irrational. She needed to consider her part in a serious crime. What had she done?

Mona told Edgar she needed to get out of the house. He wanted to go with her, but she insisted she needed time to clear her head. When her phone rang and she saw it was Detective Lane, she deleted the message and continued walking on a path through Washington Park, one of Roxbury's oldest parks. She often took her kids to this park because it offered a hub of local activities, sports and community events along with direct access to a playground, tennis and basketball courts, a swimming pool and ice-skating arena. Mona let tears fall as she remembered how little Carlos was when he played on the swings.

Will this be the last outdoor walk she would ever take? As she wandered down the path, she noticed the bright colors of autumn. She will miss that, too. Her favorite time of the year. But without Carlos, she would never experience love for a season or for anything. What had she done?

She was guilty of causing a terrible crime, and the pain she felt was because she had broken her moral code... thou shalt not kill.

Carlos had mentioned Alik and how he looked up to him. At the time, Mona knew Carlos was vulnerable and capable of being led down the wrong path by an unhealthy friendship. She tried to warn Carlos to stay away from him when she found out that Alik had a reputation for criminal and dangerous behavior. She thought he had listened to her... and the idea that Carlos might have been shot by someone he knew and looked up to, tore at her heart.

Miguel kept calling their house repeatedly to see what he could do to help. He loved Carlos like a son and Mona knew he was angry and impulsive and would do anything to get even. And then one day... when she was at her lowest... She told him about Alik Leonard and said he was the one who had killed her son. Miguel was furious that Carlos even knew a gang member. He told Mona he would take care of things.

Mona feared that if Miguel had killed Alik, she might be charged with aiding or abetting the crime. Was that possible? Now, she doubted she would ever be able to ease this emotional burden.

An hour later, as she sat on a park bench, she saw Edgar come running towards her. He was waving his hands frantically, calling out that she needed to come home. "The police just arrested Miguel! They think he murdered that kid... the one who shot Carlos!"

FRIDAY, OCTOBER 20th

The defense lawyer who was called for Miguel advised him to keep quiet and to spend a night in jail. The police were searching for evidence in his shop and car, and if they found anything he would be formally arrested. Miguel sat staring at his hands. He knew he was defeated.

When Alan arrived at the precinct, Edgar and Mona were waiting in the lobby. Their expressions were nervous and somewhat sad. "Let's go into my office," Alan said. "Can I get you anything?" Both shook their heads.

Bringing an additional chair over to his desk, Alan questioned why they were at his office this morning. Mona let out a slow breath, dragging out the moment, wondering what the consequence of telling the detective would be. Finally, Edgar spoke up, "My wife thinks she caused that kid's death. The kid who shot our son."

Alan took his time and then spoke calmly, "I need you to explain this to me step by step." He then called Sasha in to join them.

Mona began, "I encouraged Miguel to go after Alik. I told him Alik was the one who shot Carlos, and he needed to pay for it. All I thought was that he would scare him or rough him up... not kill him! But Miguel was angry and... truthfully... I wished for his death." She began to cry. "I didn't mean to..."

Alan had heard other confessions like this one. People who blamed themselves for suggesting a crime without knowing the outcome of their words. Once again, Alan asked for details. "When did you speak to Mr. Juarez about Alik?"

Mona looked confused at first, trying to think back on the conversation. "Miguel called the house a lot trying to help. I think it was after you came to the house and asked me about Alik. I was devastated. And then Miguel called... and I fell apart."

Sasha spoke up, "Mona, are you saying you told Miguel about Alik and encouraged him to do something? To get even?"

Mona shook her head and desperately tried to work out an answer in this emotionally tense situation. "No... but I'm not sure. Can I speak with Miguel?"

"Not at this time," Alan said. "Did Miguel tell you he had done something to harm Alik?"

Mona looked up. "No. I haven't spoken to him since that time." She looked to Edgar to confirm. He nodded.

Alan thought for a long minute. "Alik was killed over a week ago. We informed you he was dead, but you only now come in to tell us what you think happened. Why did you wait?"

Edgar looked defensive. "We heard Miguel was arrested! Mona can't get the idea that she was involved out of her head!"

Alan understood. Grief plays games with survivors, and they need to blame someone. He felt sorry for Mona. "Sasha, will you take a statement from Mrs. Rivera so we can have it on record."

Edgar left with the two women, but before he closed

the door he turned back to Alan. "We're just so miserable. Our hearts are broken." Alan understood.

Lieutenant Johnson knocked on the door and entered. "What was that all about?"

Alan grimaced. "We have a suspect in jail for questioning in reference to Alik Leonard's death, and now Carlos Rivera's parents think they might have encouraged this guy to murder him. It's a wait and see situation."

"Anything newer on the Murphy gun?"

"Detective Collins is searching Caleb's phone to track down misleading communications. She thinks the perps were hackers who try to find out when families are away so they can rob their homes. If this is true, we may be on to something bigger than suspected."

"Well... it looks like Tom's name might get out, then. I hope he's ready. Let me know what you find."

Alan watched as Johnson walked out of the room and hoped the Murphys understood or appreciated how much time they were putting into this case.

It would be a while until forensics got back with details from the search of Juarez's car and shop. Not wanting to waste time, Alan called over to the team to see if they suspected anything so far. Ralph Taylor answered the call. "Yes, Detective, we have samples of blood in his car and in a supply room. If it matches your guy and the victim, we'll have the answer soon."

Sasha knocked on Alan's door and walked in. "Do you want me to keep the Riveras here or let them return home?"

"What do you think? Was there any evidence that Mona coerced Juarez into committing murder?"

"Not really. She feels guilty, though. I think she needs

to go to the doctor and maybe get some meds. She hasn't been sleeping and seems confused. Should I let them go?"

"Sure. But tell them to stay close by, not to leave the city."

Alan realized this could all be an error in judgement. Maybe both murders were accidents. Why would Alik kill someone who admired him and why would Juarez kill someone if he only wanted to scare him? Alan still hadn't located the two other teens present when the gun went off and killed Carlos. He decided to call Piece Leonard and ask a few more questions.

Pierce was on the phone with the funeral parlor when Alan called. When he was finished with the call, he noticed that Alan had left a voicemail. "I'm sorry to bother you again, but I have a quick question if you have a minute."

Pierce took a deep breath and shook his head. What now? He was done talking with the police. His phone rang again. "What is it?" he yelled into the receiver.

Alan heard the anger and decided to proceed cautiously. "Mr. Leonard, did you ever locate the two teens who were with your nephew when Carlos was shot? Because I'm looking at a possible theory that may indicate the incident was an accident." Alan paused to let this sink in. "I learned that Carlos and Alik knew each other and didn't have any sort of disagreement. And another thought, did Alik even know how to use a gun?"

Pierce was surprised by the concern he heard in Alan's voice. "As far as I knew, Alik didn't have any experience with guns. But I can't be certain. I didn't keep track of him all the time. I had my gun well hidden, even though he found it. And I can't even tell you when it went missing."

"We heard he used the gun for intimidation around the stores and robbing people at night. But no one has reported his gun going off. I need to ask the two teens if shooting Carlos was maybe an accident."

Pierce rummaged through his desk until he found what he was looking for.. "I know a kid by the name of Jamal Lewis who hung out with Alik. He probably knows something."

"Have you spoken with him?"

"Not yet. I never considered it might all be a stupid accident."

Alan took the name and said he would get back to him.

Officer Rosen was getting ready for his assignment of the day when Alan called. "Detective, what can I do for you?"

"I have a name of a friend of Alik Leonard's that I wonder if you recognize… it's Jamal Lewis. Sound familiar?"

Rosen thought for a second. "I think I saw his name on the gym roster when Detective Lane and I picked up the gym bag. They had a list of names who owed past dues, and he was on it. Do you want me to follow up?"

"That would be great. Can you get this done soon?"

"I'll go right now. My Captain is still okay with my helping you."

Alan was pleased with the cooperation. Police days are often long and filled with a variety of tasks filled with new challenges. The fact that Officer Rosen was willing to add another responsibility to his schedule was appreciated. "Thank you. Call me if you can locate Lewis."

Alan's next job was to find out more about the investigation of Miguel Juarez car and shop. He called down to forensics and was told the report was on its way. He then got word that Miguel's lawyer wanted to talk. But first, Alan wanted to read the report.

Sure enough, Alik's blood was a match found in Miguel's shop and car. When the lawyer arrived, Alan had all the evidence he needed.

The lawyer began, "I have advised Juarez to talk with you and tell you what happened. He is waiting."

Alan nodded. "Let's go." On the way out the door he motioned for Sasha to join them.

Miguel looked resigned. He slumped in his chair and his eyes stared at the metal table. Alan formally introduced himself and Sasha and then turned on the recorder. "Mr. Juarez, tell us what happened on the night of Wednesday, October 11th. Did you meet with Alik Leonard?"

Miguel looked up at the detectives and nodded his head. "Yes, I did," he said quietly. "I asked him to come around... told him I had a job he might want." He then hit the table with his right hand. "I just wanted to talk to him! But he was playing this real tough guy and started disrespecting me... and so I asked him if he was the one who shot Carlos, and he laughed at me!" Miguel shook his head and slammed his fist on the table. "I lost it! I punched him just to shut him up! And he kept fighting back so I hit him again... and again..." Miguel started to sob. "I've never done that before... hit someone so hard! I didn't mean to... I lost it!"

Alan looked at the lawyer and decided to stop the interview. They had what they needed. He left Sasha to take a final statement.

Once again, a senseless murder, a crime of passion. It might end up being tried as temporary insanity or provocation. Alan knew that the media followed cases like this and spent an inordinate amount of time speculating on how a guilty sentence might end up reducing the charge to manslaughter instead of first-degree murder. The media was a powerful tool in raising awareness, especially one involving teens. But it will be up to the lawyers and judges who will decide.

In the meantime, Alan would have to let Pierce and Ella Leonard know that Miguel had confessed.

Officer Rosen had left a message when Alan returned to his office. He had located Jamal Lewis and wanted to know how to proceed. Alan called him immediately. "Where is he?"

"At the moment he's at home, in an apartment on 4th next to the Roxbury Center. Do you want me to go talk with him?"

"Wait for me there. I want to hear what he has to say."

Twenty minutes later Alan and Rosen were knocking on the apartment door. It was a run-down unit that was probably on the verge of being condemned, but people still paid rent to live there. Rosen called out, "Police, open the door!"

A kid no older than eight slowly opened the door and stared at the two men. Alan spoke up, "Is your brother Jamal at home?"

The kid nodded. "I'll get him."

Two minutes later a very sleepy looking teen came to the door, "What you want?"

Alan put his hand on the door. "Just a minute of your time. You're not in trouble, but we have a few questions about your friend Alik Leonard."

Jamal looked worried but stepped out onto the landing. "What about him?"

"We heard you were with him when he shot Carlos Rivera. Tell us what happened."

Jamal stepped back and folded his arms. "Look, Alik didn't even know how to shoot that gun! It just went off and then he threw it away! We were all scared and ran... we saw the kid drop... it wasn't supposed to happen!"

Alan slowly shook his head. "Why didn't you come forward and tell us what you witnessed?"

Jamal shook his head rapidly. "And then what? Be charged with something I didn't even do or know what was going to happen? I know how you cops like to blame us..."

"Okay. That's all we needed to know." Alan then had another thought. He reached into his pocket and pulled out a business card for Carla's Center. "If you need some direction, call this lady. She can help."

Alan thanked Rosen for his quick work and then drove to speak with Pierce and Ella Leonard. When he walked in the building, he saw Pierce waiting by the elevator. "Is it fixed?" Alan asked with a smile.

"Finally. Why are you back?"

"We have someone in custody for Alik's murder. I wanted to tell you and his grandmother to put your minds at rest."

Pierce looked skeptical and then looked down at the floor. "I guess I'm appreciative, Detective, but it won't bring him back. He was on a destructive path, but I always hoped he would get his life together, get a job, and start acting like a man."

"Do you want me to go with you to tell his grandmother that we have a suspect?"

Pierce shook his head. "No, I'll take care of it." He put out his hand to shake. "Thank you, Detective."

Alan shook hands and turned and walked away. Pierce was a good man. He would remind Carla to check in with the project and see what she could offer.

Before he returned to the office, Alan decided to walk through the Commons and clear his head. He knew that as hard as people try to insulate themselves, we are all human and fallible. Accidents often happen, and unexpected or unforeseen circumstances can result in injury or even death. Carlos Rivera and Alik Leonard were victims of senseless attacks.

Alan waited for a light to change and looked up at the high-rise apartment building across the street from the Boston Common. He noticed there was a written sign posted for an available unit and decided to take a look. The two-bedroom unit was 1,374 square feet and was located on the twelfth floor. It had a waterfront view of the canals from Massachusetts Bay and a partial view of Government Center. It boasted being steps away from the Commons and close to shops, restaurants, parks and public transportation. Alan didn't have to look around to see that the description was true to the location.

What would it be like living in a high-rise building? Besides the spectacular views, Alan supposed there was a sense of isolation once you get up that high. You wouldn't be able to hear the noise of the city, but would you be aware of construction that reached the heights these days? He also imagined that the wind was stronger the higher up you got.

Did that make the air quality better?

Shaking his head, Alan wondered who could pay the $6000 monthly rent. There were amenities, of course, like 24/7 surveillance, a fitness center and rooftop pool. But did the residents understand they were dependent on the elevator? This might be a problem when having to evacuate the building. Do people consider this?

He put the notice in his pocket and walked away. He would never consider living in a high-rise.

Detective Collins was waiting for Alan at his office door. "Sir, I think the Murphy case is over."

Alan followed her into his office and offered her a chair. "What do you mean... over?"

"Well, sir, Tom and Sheila Murphy have decided to let the media know that a gun was found at their house. They will explain why the gun was there and ask for understanding." Vivian looked at Alan for a response.

"Go on."

"They are worried that Caleb will keep being targeted and since his phone is now in police hands, they hope the criminals will be caught. It's been handed over to tech."

"Have you informed Lieutenant Johnson about that?"

"Yes, sir. He thinks it's a good idea. Mr. Murphy is willing to go public on this so that takes the blame off the police. Well... not that the blame was there... but you know how these things turn on you." Vivian looked hopeful that Alan agreed with her.

"Good job, Detective. Is there anything else?"

Vivian thought for a full minute. "I appreciate you letting me handle this case, Sir. I want to learn more about how computers are used to solve crimes. I hope I'll be assigned to more of these types of cases." Vivian stood and saluted, even though it wasn't required.

Alan scanned his desk that was laden with files. So many time-consuming tasks lay before him. Sitting back in his chair, he hated to think about the expensive benefits he might lose if he retired. Sick days, lunch hours, health insurance, vacations… was he ready to give these things up? Alan knew he was an achiever at heart. He needed to be engaged in something that contributed to his job or his life. Why was it so hard for him to do nothing? He always seemed to have something on his mind, and he liked knowing he was totally involved with a project. He looked at the time and decided to talk this over with Maggie.

Maggie listened to Alan talk once more about retiring. She stopped him. "Alan, when was the last time you had a real vacation? I mean a real get away."

Alan had to think about it. When he was married, they had taken eight-year-old Sam to Disneyland once. That was a complete disaster because it rained the whole three days that they visited the magic kingdom. Then there was the time he attended a conference in Hawaii, and he got such a bad sunburn he almost needed to be hospitalized.

"I can only remember vacations as being a lot of work with no special memory or desire to return."

"That seems sad to me, Alan. I've been on so many wonderful vacations that I consider them to be essential to my happiness. Let's plan something and see if I can change your mind about going away."

Alan agreed but secretly hoped it would be a long time coming. He thought about vacations as doing nothing or not being engaged in a purpose like learning, developing, figuring something out. It made him feel anxious just thinking about it. "Okay, where should we go?"

Three weeks later...

Alan had only one more loose end to tie up before catching the 9:15 and saying goodbye to the city for a while. He was meeting Maggie at the airport and then they were on their way for a real vacation. They had agreed that Florida was not their cup of tea and decided to throw caution to the wind and fly to Greece. They both felt the urge to experience a place and culture that had jaw dropping ancient sites, crystal clear waters and picturesque scenery. Everyone who went praised the Greek cuisine for its fresh ingredients, bold flavors and simple preparations. Greece was also the home of many wineries and breweries, not to mention the Greek coffee with the added touch of cinnamon.

They both hoped it was true that the Greek hospitality was warm and welcoming. Everyone said they will feel a great sense of ease and relief because they will be treated with great kindness by the locals.

Alan sent his retirement paperwork to HR the week before. He's nervous about what the future will look like when he returns from vacation. He was given a grand retirement celebration and even an Apple watch. As soon as he learned how to work the darn thing and make it stop sending him messages, he might be comfortable trying some other novel ideas.

He smiled.